Praise for the Stories of Consigned to the Sea

"The best of the book for me was [...] *In the Runes* by Danielle Ackley-McPhail, a story of the last dragon hunting down the runes that contain the life forces of young dragons, waiting to be born. —Rebecca Gomez, Goodreads

"*In The Runes* by Danielle Ackley-McPhail [...] tempted me with some intriguing settings and vividly drawn characters. —Lindsey Duncan, GoodReads

"Dripping with tension, *Consigned To The Sea* is a powerful tale with interesting twists toward the end and a strong lead. Recommended." —Bryan Thomas Schmidt, Rise Reviews

Other Titles
by Danielle Ackley-McPhail

THE ETERNAL CYCLE TRILOGY
Yesterday's Dreams
Tomorrow's Memories
Today's Promise

Eternal Wanderings

A BAD-ASS FAERIE TALE SERIES
The Halfling's Court
The Redcaps' Queen
The High King's Fool
(forthcoming)

Baba Ali and the Clockwork Djinn
co-written by Day Al-Mohamed

Daire's Devils

Literary Handyman
Build-A-Book Workshop
More Tips From the Handyman

A Legacy of Stars
Dawns a New Day
Transcendence
The Fox's Fire
The Kindly One

The Die Is Cast
co-written with Mike McPhail

CONSIGNED TO THE SEA

DANIELLE ACKLEY-McPHAIL

PAPER PHOENIX PRESS

Pennsville, NJ

PUBLISHED BY
Paper Phoenix Press
A division of eSpec Books
PO Box 493
Stratford, NJ 08084
www.paperphoenixpress.com
www.especbooks.com

ISBN: 978-1-942990-52-9
ISBN (ebook): 978-1-942990-53-6

Interior Art: Fotolia.com
Wave Border © xelena
Rope Ornaments. Decorative Design Elements.© pilarts
Jolly Roger © lina0486
Girl © okalinichenko
Mermaid © TIMURA
Viking Longship Sailing B © xunantunich
Otary - Otarie © Erica Guilane-Nachez

Copyeditor: Greg Schauer
Interior Design: Danielle McPhail, Sidhe na Daire Multimedia
www.sidhenadaire.com

To my husband, Mike McPhail,
who is often consigned to waiting
while I discover these fantastic worlds

Acknowledgements

Thank you (in order of appearance) to Valerie Griswold-Ford, Brenda Cooper, D.B. Jackson, Misty Massey, and Alma Alexander for generously donating their time to write introductions for this collection. To each of you, your friendship and support mean very much to me.

"In the Runes" originally published in *Rum and Runestones*, edited by Valerie Griswold-Ford, Dragon Moon Press, 2011
"To Reach for Distant Shores" originally published in *Mermaids 13*, edited by John L. French, Padwolf Publishing, 2012
"Sweet Liam Roanes" Previously published in *No Longer Dreams*, edited by Danielle Ackley-McPhail, L. Jagi Lamplighter, Lee C. Hillman, and Jeff Lyman, Lite Circle Books, 2005
"Consigned to the Sea" originally published in *Sails and Sorcery*, edited by W.H. Horner, Fantasist Enterprises, 2007
"By Silent Spell Caught" originally published in *Spells and Swashbucklers*, edited by Valerie Griswold-Ford, Dragon Moon Press, 2012

Contents

Introduction

THERE'S SOMETHING HYPNOTIC ABOUT THE SEA: THE WAVES, moving rhythmically over a surface that is alternately dark and bright, whispering long after midnight and singing in the midday sun. You never know what is lurking just under the surface, or traveling on the swells, but you can taste the salt and the magic in the air.

In the same way that the sea lulls you, brings you into its embrace, and drags you beneath the waves, good stories can wrap their words around you, drowning you in images and filling your senses. When you find good stories about the sea, you've found gold.

And that's what this collection is: sea-gold, full of magic and promise. Dani (I get to call her that, since I've had the pleasure of editing two stories of hers) has gathered together four tales of the sea that sparkle with magic. Selkies, dragons, mermaids, and

pirates stalk through these pages, dragging you along with them.

"In the Runes" and "By Silent Spell Caught" are from her *Tales of the Last Celdraig* series, speaking of Camriel, the daughter of the last dragon of the world, who has been sent to collect the dragon eggs from the men who would use them as spellstones. This use unwittingly (or perhaps not) kills the dragonlings inside, and Camriel will stop at nothing to save them. Her mission may be in jeopardy, but help will come from a most unlikely ally.

"Consigned to the Sea" looks at the dark side of sea magic, and the myth of the selkie, as the unnamed narrator deals with pirates bent on destroying her and her young daughter. This is not a tale for the faint of heart, but trust me, it's worth it. And considering I'm a pirate, that's saying something—I was rooting for the mother, not the pirate captain.

And "To Reach for Distant Shores" explores the fascination that those who live in the sea have with us, and with the things they cannot experience, or explain. One mermaid's ardent wish to understand what she sees in the sky brings her into a situation that she could not have imagined.

Each of these stories will bring you into a world that you couldn't have realized existed, and all of them are bound by the sea. I hope you enjoy them as much as I did.

—Val Griswold-Ford
author of the *Dark Horseman* series and
editor of *Rum and Runstones* and
Spells and Swashbucklers

In the Runes

A Tale of the Last Celdraig

T HE WAVES PUMMELED THE SHORE AS THE LONGBOAT WENT TO ground. The sharp bite of salt—with a fainter hint of decay from flotsam—flavored the air and the timbers creaked as they left the cradle of the sea to settle on land. Three men remained sitting while the rest of the mates scrambled to pull the vessel more firmly onto the beach. The scrape of sand against salt-soaked wood accompanied their low grunts and the moon cast their soft shadows across the shore like the writhing ghosts of great hunched beasts.

"You will wait here, Morrow, until we reach halfway to the trees, then follow," ordered Captain Tulo, the man with the short braid of dark brown hair trailing down his neck. "Do not come within fifteen feet of us with your mumbling or I will cut your tongue from your head."

Morrow nodded but did not flinch as the two men moved off, the mate, Cragg, with a spade over his shoulder, and the captain clutching a burlap sack the size of a small ham. The runecaster did not even stand until they'd traveled halfway across the prescribed expanse. The moment they passed it he set off, keeping both pace and distance, his lips moving in a barely heard invocation, his expression serene despite the recent threat.

The captain did not mean it, surely. Morrow was good, but he was useless without his tongue; his runecasting required him to vocalize, which was better than most, who must sketch the marks on air, water, or even paper, to work the 'cast. Very few had the skill or the strength to do so purely with the mind. Or, more accurately perhaps, the focus for it. Yes, Morrow had no illusions: he was better than most, but not all. And any of their kind were rare. He considered himself safe from the captain, though, mostly because he was not stupid. He held a raw gemstone, roughly the size and shape of a small lime; he was knowledgeable enough of his craft that only the jewel in his hand would be imprinted by his 'casting.

Letting the tug of his magic flowing into the stone soothe him, the runecaster followed Captain Tulo and Cragg, the only other sailor trusted with the secret of the runestones. Technically he was first mate, but the captain was stingy with his power and none aboard the *Devil's Get* held any rank that they did not earn — and keep — amongst themselves. Morrow had only to think of the razor-sharp collar about his own neck to be reminded of the captain's ruthlessness. The runes holding the edge from his flesh were placed there — clearly — by another, as Morrow would not have enslaved himself. They could be spoken away by Tulo at any time, from any distance. Someday Morrow would find his way past the binding, until then he behaved as the model runecaster.

Ahead he noticed the others slowing and adjusted his steps accordingly, all the while murmuring the runes that imprinted their path into the stone. Once he completed the spell, the captain — or anyone else given the trigger word — would have the means to find the future treasure they buried this night.

The breeze ruffled Morrow's hair and sandy soil shifted beneath his feet as he followed the pirates. A sudden chittering high in the palm fronds to his left made him jump, but he took care to keep his voice steady and constant as he spoke the runes. With his hindbrain he readied his defense, should more than monkeys or song birds come down from the trees. Of all the spells he knew, this was the strongest and the most closely guarded; passed down to him by his granddame, known by none but those counted as a part of his family. He dared think that 'casting would protect him from even god or devil, were they small enough. Spell in place but for the speaking, Morrow brought his attention back to his task.

Ahead, the captain and first mate stopped, the latter lowering the spade. Morrow ended his runecasting well before the distance the captain dictated, the path to the clearing complete and a reversing end-rune added, binding the return path to mirror the way in. The stone was now spelled to lead to and from this spot for as long as the strength of the rune lasted, though looking around, he could not imagine why anyone would do so. It was pretty enough, but what was the likelihood there would be much of a harvest here? Yet the captain claimed the place was regularly used by rune-witches from a nearby island. Maybe, maybe not. It scarcely mattered to Morrow. The pirates would bury their cache of stones and any spell worked in their vicinity would be captured in the closest runestone at the moment of its casting, with the witches none the wiser that they hadn't merely misspoken the spell, as sometimes happened. They would leave this clearing ignorant of the theft.

The thought soured in Morrow's mind, he having had more than just a spell snatched away. It galled that the pirates turned his efforts against others of his kind. No matter, though; he bore no responsibility for anything more than his "muttering." 'Twas the captain that stole the runecasting of others, not Morrow, though not all would see it so. Some would call him a traitor. Let them. He had little choice for he liked his skin too much for it to part on principle. From the day he woke with a shiny new collar after 'casting a protection rune on a pouch for a customer, this had been his involuntary life. But he watched and tested and someday he'd be free. For now, he did as instructed.

"It is done, 'caster?" Tulo called out, adjusting his coat as the first mate began to dig.

"Aye, sir," Morrow answered, stepping forward, runestone held out. It glowed softly with the magic of his casting.

The captain looked at it and gave a familiar smirk with a hint of a sneer in it. The first mate stopped digging. He straightened, then raised the blade of the shovel, a grin revealing teeth gone yellow and breath flavored with rum. Morrow looked back to the captain. Confusion reshaped his features. And still he could not believe...

Then he dropped the runestone as the jungle erupted around him. The underbrush thrashed, as did the fronds overhead. Yells sounded close by, the men's voices echoed as demons' howls in Morrow's heart, and before he could duck away a hard shove sent him forward and to his knees, closer to the captain and Cragg. He reflexively uttered the runes of his defensive spell as a blow took him between the shoulders.

Nothing.

A second clipped the base of his skull, another, his kidneys, none with a killing force, though brutal enough. He curled as best he could and frantically muttered the rune again, and again, all his will and arcane strength behind it. Still nothing. He kept muttering brokenly until a familiar tugging registered with his addled mind. His eyes went wide and his body chilled, shaking as a kick jarred him loose from his ball. He angled a horrified glance toward the sack of stones. Stones he'd already set with Tulo's trigger words. They glowed faintly through the burlap, confirming his master's betrayal even as Tulo spoke *that* word and the runes about Morrow's neck faded.

He felt the bite of cold steel as the collar closed on his flesh.

There was no more muttering. Morrow stared up at the empty palm fronds, rigid with horror, until Tulo leaned over him, obstructing his view. Then the runecaster floated free, looking down on his empty shell and the man that murdered him, senses intact, though muffled and without substance. He existed as a shadow, but he could hear and see as Tulo mocked him.

"There are a half-dozen like you in every port," the captain said with disdain as Morrow's soul began to drift.

Hatred supplanted horror.

The pirates laughed and sang coarse songs as they went away with a sack of stones imprinted with his family's blast rune.

Morrow felt himself fade as the breeze pushed at him.

He panicked. Reached out. Latched his thoughts on the dropped runestone, which lay forgotten on the ground, tumbled beneath the undergrowth. His magic, his essence, still warmed it with a faint glow. He felt a familiar tugging.

A dragon rode the thermals lacing the tropic sky. Her belly gently mottled in shifting patterns that mimicked her backdrop, complete with starbright glimmers from the occasional diamond scale mixed among those midnight blue, deep amethyst, and sapphire, her wings bowed and billowed like the surrounding wisps of night clouds as the air cooled. She circled in lazy arcs, her neck craning, her gaze sweeping the far-below shore. Faceted eyes narrowed, the earthfire kindling in their depths. A snarl like thunder shook her throat as in her heart she felt the fading echo of as much as a score of emberlings even now moved beyond her reach.

Her belly roiled with an unvoiced scream but she locked her muzzle shut on it. Let mankind dream and wonder, tell their terrible tales around the bottle and the bar, let them scurry from doorpost to arch, but never must they know for certain that dragons were born from more than foolishness, or whiskey vapors and bad beef. If that knowledge were common, she and the dragons that would one day rise from the emberlings she succeeded in returning to their earthfire nests would be hunted down and their flames banished. She shuddered at the horror of that thought.

Camirel stilled her cry and searched on. With a desperate hope, she let her eyes sweep the land below once more, reaching out with will and wish for some sign any emberling yet remained. Ear ridges lifted and fanned, a scarlet frill feathering an elegant head shaped somewhat like an antelope, delicate despite the massive size. Swiveling, the ridges confirmed what her flicking tongue already tasted on the air: no human heartbeat pulsed within a league, though primates peered at her from the tallest palms below, cowering beneath the fronds. Lower she swooped and they scattered, chittering through the trees and into the brush, revealing what had been too faint for her to sense. In the heart of the islet jungle laid a tiny, muted spark.

Triumph was much harder to rein in than rage.

Cami didn't bother, belling as she soared down from the sky, skimming surf and sand until bronze claws gripped the anchoring reef bared by low tide. There was no one nearby. She lay herself down upon the rock, curving muzzle to flank, and breathed with the rhythm of the waves, let herself cool, then gently pushed the earthfire back below to cradle in the deep pumice hollow her draconic senses told her was there. A shudder. A ripple. Then the magic currents snapped.

She rose on two legs. Moonlight briefly glimmered off of naked flesh the next moment clothed in a loose, dark cotton robe. She murmured no rune, etched none in sand or water or air; thought simply became fact. Camirel had always been gifted that way. More so since her rebirth. The young woman thought no more of it as she hurried unerringly through the brush, her hand going through a slit in the side of the robe to an empty pouch bound around her waist. It never left her person, not even during the change, thanks to the spell she'd wrought on the leather. Its emptiness weighed heavily on her. But perhaps with fortune's blessing it would not be empty long.

Striding faster, following a trail of broken foliage, along the way she passed two large lizards fighting over the carcass of a man. The remains were much abused, but around his throat she spied a glint of metal sunk into the skin clear around, like a necklace gone too tight. Her own throat tightened in sympathy until a hiss called her attention back to the scaled contenders. The lizards had united, scurrying forward to force her away. The emberling hard in her thoughts, Cami took no convincing at all to leave the brutal sight.

Once more hurrying through the brush, she soon came to a nearby clearing disturbed by digging, lizard tracks…and violence —though no sign remained, beyond a few crushed ferns and a darkened patch of damp soil that smelled coppery even to her lesser nose. She closed her eyes. Shut out the signs of disturbance. Shut out the memory of the poor soul she'd passed on the trail. She stilled her thoughts and turned a slow circle, letting her heart seek the glimmer too weak for her mortal sight to see. There was a flicker, like heat lightning. Its glow too slight for her to latch onto. The circling stopped.

Cami shook off frustration and let her head fall back until her throat straightened and her closed eyes angled toward the sky. Deep breaths brought calm to her heart while the warm island breeze riffled her hair. Around her, the jungle sang a lullaby full of *sushing* fronds and sleepy monkey sounds. She let it calm her further until not one muscle remained tense and her legs sank her to the sandy soil. Head still back, she let her tongue trill against her teeth, echoing deep in her throat, blending with the night-song until it carried her call to the one she sought.

Interference muffled the resonance, the earthfire dim, but Cami felt it like a weak sunbeam against her neck, slightly off to the left. Her head lowered and turned, her eyes opening languidly until a nearby gleam winked at her from the underbrush. Slinking forward, she stared intently at the gemstone hidden beneath a leaf the size of her head. To the unknowing it appeared as any other uncut jewel, only rather larger than most. To a runecaster, or any other in tune with the earthfire, it was something magical, but nothing more. To Cami—adopted daughter of the Last Mother—it was a dragon egg stolen from the earth much before its time.

She frowned. Something troubled her about this emberling.

A sullen glow emanated from the stone's heart. Almost as if she stared at the ember through a haze of smoke or shadow, roiling and dark, smothering. Perhaps the Last Mother would have known what was wrong, but she was gone. Not for the first time, Cami cursed the fact that she had nothing left to guide her but instinct.

In this, she remained conflicted.

The thought of gripping the stone made the skin of her palm ripple and twitch away from the wrongness she sensed. Yet this was her sacred charge: to find and reclaim the embers of the earthfire, to return them to their molten nest deep within the First Mother that they may learn and grow and rise from below the earth to sing their songs, restoring true dragons to the world.

Her duty was stronger than her doubt.

Her fingers closed around the cool, dark stone, felt etching upon the surface, and this time her whole body arched, her grip tightening until the rough edges cut her flesh and the swirling chaos of death slashed at her mind.

Cami fell senseless to the jungle floor.

"Haul anchor and away!" the captain bellowed before the longboat even cleared the rail. He leapt to the deck, the heavy heat of the sack thumping his back. The masts and timbers creaked as pirates scurried into the rigging and the ship yawed with the pounding of the surf against the hull. Tulo shifted his stride with the pitch as he went to secure the stones. At the door of his cabin he uttered a word to turn the knob; another locked it secure behind him. Inside, guided by the sunlight streaming through the windows of his cabin, he immediately carried his burden across the chamber to a chest beside his bunk. It was made of thick cypress planks bound around and anchored to the floor with heavy bars of iron. A different word, barely whispered, lifted the lid on a small cache of assorted stones, no more than eight, three gleaming rubies spelled for healing, and five other mixed stones each bearing a different set of runes: one for light, one for causing pain, the emerald held a death curse, and the last two summoned wind for the sails. All captured runes, none of them as powerful as the twelve newest, each and every stone etched with the legendary blast rune known only by Morrow's line. A priceless treasure indeed, with pending war whispered of in every port.

Without the sack, the inside of the chest revealed more bare wood than rough gems. This night's work brought his total to twenty, for the sacrifice of but one; more than enough to fill the coffer with gold coin several times over. He would dole out a few runestones once they reached Phiron; not too many, or it was worth his life. For a rare few and the promise of more, Devon and his hag would pay; for a haul like this they would do violence and take them, much as he had with Morrow. Tulo stowed the stones and brought down the heavy lid, binding word spoken before the thud ended.

He whistled as he returned to deck, already planning a trip to port. Wine and women and gold to be had…oh, and a new runecaster. Idly he caressed the pommel of his dagger, where a smallish runestone nested, nearly hidden by gold filigree. No, mustn't forget the 'caster.

"Cragg, set course for Phiron."

A mass cheer went up from the rigging.

Cami woke to a monkey tugging at her hand. He grumbled and shrieked alternately, prying at her fingers in a manner that should have snapped them, then yanked at her arm as if that might instead come free. Summoning a flicker of earthfire, Camirel growled with her dragon voice.

Such screaming she had never heard. The creature—and its more timid companions in the trees—fled. The screaming continued, echoing in her mind. Still linked to the earthfire, Cami sniffed and probed, searched for any sign, any at all, that she was not alone. Plant life and decay were plentiful; as were the monkeys. But, other than a scattering of birds and reptiles, nothing else drew breath on the islet. Slow and careful she set the emberling on the ground before her and stared at it intently. Unlike the others she had found before this, it was marred, changed. Something etched the surface and clouded its heart. The Last Mother had said to bring *all* emberlings, but she'd not warned any could be tainted. Cami did not know what to do. She had reclaimed so few; which was the greater risk, taking this one, damaged as it might be, or not?

Don't stare. The words sounded in her head, gruff and masculine, tinged with ill-concealed unease.

With a squeal that morphed into a growl, Cami drew harder upon the earthfire, and rose to a crouch. The cotton robe she'd magically donned earlier now barely contained her; she changed with the sudden heat of the 'fire until a half-human, half-dragon melding loomed above the emberling, with human arms and legs and the beginnings of a dragon's muzzled head beneath the sweep of her dark gold hair. Jewel-scaled skin reflecting the colors of the jungle wrapped her flesh like armor.

Again, the screaming in her head.

An odd muttering followed the sound, until Cami felt a faint ripple, as if someone attempted to draw upon mage energy, but nothing came of it. The glow at the heart of the emberling flared and pulsed in time with the muttering. She had felt death's touch before, shocking and brutal, unyielding, as the Last Mother sacrificed herself for Camirel. She felt it now at the heart of the stone, a second soul disconnected from the earthfire.

"Hush," she hissed softly, aloud, her voice faintly reminiscent of the lizards that had been fighting over what must have been his body. Cami loosened her grip on the earthfire until only the protective scales remained, sheathing her own form. The anger she could not so simply let go. A shudder rippled her skin and her hands flexed until short, curved talons capped the tips of her fingers, as instinctively she drew the earthfire close once more. The dead had no rightful place among the young. That such had touched the tender emberling…who knew what effect that would have?

"You have taken a place not yours."

A sense of hesitation as the glow flickered wildly.

I did not mean to. I did not know. I'm sorry…I cannot say how it is even possible…

"You have mutilated and scarred our young," she growled—for Cami spoke also with the echo of the First Mother when earthfire filled her.

The gem flared, then dimmed to a bare glow. It seemed to tremble against her hand as she picked it up and stared at the runes etched into the surface. What effect would they have if she nested the emberling? The runes themselves could wreak havoc, let alone the sundered soul.

Young?

Camirel did not answer. Secrecy in this had been a part of the song she'd absorbed before her rebirth, along with the knowledge all dragons shared from the inception of their kind until the death of it. Both were vital if she was to resurrect the species, but was this unseated being any kind of threat to that? Hard to say; she could end him easily enough, though at the sacrifice of the emberling…she still could not say if that would be a bad thing. *Perhaps it was worth the risk,* she thought. *If the usurper had knowledge of the others.*

"This stone you are in," she said, her voice low and as sharp as her talons. "There were others here. Where have they gone?"

Silence met her question.

"Do not think to lie. I can sense they were here."

I do not intend to…I do not know…*but…* The man's thoughts held an edge of guilt, his presence strengthened as he thought the matter through. *Tulo, the captain of the* Devil's Get, *he will not horde such a treasure long. If he heads anywhere, it will be to Phiron. 'Tis his preferred port and we…we have been quite a while at sea.*

Cami's heart quickened and she felt the earthfire answer as she called upon her dragon nature. Before she changed completely she deposited the stone into the pouch just as the change sank it beneath scaled hide.

What were you called, man?

The voice remained silent, as if it searched for the answer. She sensed his confusion and felt pity for him. Death was indeed unsettling.

Morrow, m'lady, he finally answered, subdued. Still suspicious of him, she did not return the favor. "M'lady" would serve nicely, though it was far above her current station.

To Phiron, then, Morrow, she thought toward the stone with fiery vehemence. Then she launched herself into the sky, leaving below screaming monkeys, churned earth, and felled trees.

The Whiskey Cask was not your typical dockside haunt. It was quiet and dark, and several streets over from the main concourse. No women served up drinks or themselves; no rousing shanty songs disturbed the night. Cragg leaned alone against the bar, more staring at a pint of ale than drinking it. Captain Tulo sat at a table in the far corner, beside the hearth, the remains of a plain meal and a full bottle of whiskey before him, but his eye on the door.

Another hour passed before it opened. The man that walked in seemed too clean and hale for the common clothing he wore. A smile on his smooth face even revealed a full set of teeth. As if any man on the docks had any such thing…or reason to smile, without a doxie to hand. Tulo would have laughed if he weren't so furious. He had waited hours. Devon played at subterfuge as if necks would not be stretched if they were caught. The fool.

Now, entering behind him, hunched and sloven and looking much more attuned to the atmosphere of the docks, the hag Zia drew a much more respectful look from Tulo. Perhaps she played as well, but she had an air about her that spoke of cunning and power. If she played, it was to a purpose. Tulo stood and made a show of drawing out a chair for her, meeting her disturbing yellow eyes as if they did not unsettle him. She gave a shrill laugh and made a show of settling into the seat, more grace in the act than Tulo would have thought her capable.

"The stones," Devon said as he settled into his own seat, hand already held out across the table, his eyes gleaming eagerly. He spoke low, his words carrying just enough for them alone to hear.

Tulo laughed at him with equal softness. Dangerously.

"Come now, I don't have them with me any more than you have the coin you would pay me with on your person." The captain sat back in a show of calculated insolence, his lip faintly sneering as his voice emphasized the word 'pay.'

Devon again betrayed his noble birth, straightening with well-exercised offense and entitlement, hand reaching for the pistol surely beneath his coat. Such weapons were costly, pretentious, and nowhere as reliable as steel or magic.

Before tempers won out, the hag's ritually scarred hand darted out to smack the lordling's down. "Don't be a fool." Her voice crackled with age, but her words had strength behind them. "What proof have you then, rogue?"

Tulo pulled a scrap of parchment from his pocket and spread it across the table. The crumpled sheet bore a carbon rubbing of one of the stones, only partial, but enough that the rune for Morrow's clan was clearly evident.

The hag nodded as Devon seethed beside her. She ignored him. "Fair enough," she said to Tulo. "And terms?"

He refolded the parchment and slid it away, then leaned forward. He looked toward Devon, who, after all, held the purse. "For the three I can give you, one hundred gold each."

"I am reminded of the difference between a thief and a pirate now," Devon said in a tight voice. "The thief robs you in secret, the pirate, face to face."

"It is not my war," Tulo answered. "I merely thought to aid where I am able. If this is too costly for you, I am sure there are others that would be grateful of my…assistance."

"Three are hardly worth my time." Devon affected a dismissive pose, good at the play when he bothered to take it seriously.

Tulo held back the smile the comment drew. He had him. "Well, I have but three right now, but I can secure more over time, should they be of use to you…."

Devon's eyes went bright and he unconsciously, barely perceptibly, leaned forward. "More?"

"A few."

"Done!" Devon forgot putting on airs in his excitement. "And where shall we collect?"

"Why, tomorrow is market day, is it not?" Tulo grinned and took a swig from the whisky bottle now that the deal was set. "I'll have a man bartering wares near the dock entrance to the market square. Hand him this mark," — the captain laid a blue-painted chip between them on the table — "and ask to see his war god carvings.

"Have the payment in full," Tulo advised. "Even should you somehow manage to make off with them, the stones are useless without the trigger word, and that you must have from me."

Devon's face flushed and his brow furrowed as he came to his feet. Before he could speak, the hag rose as well, drawing Devon down by the collar of his coat. She murmured low in his ear as she nodded and led the noble out the door.

The pirate captain laughed and capped his bottle. "They are so amusing when they scheme, they'll have a shock though, if they try to play the pirate at his own game. Come, let's find some place a bit more rousing," he said to his man, and they too departed.

The timbers of the masts creaked and swayed as the dragon circled high over head stirring the winds. Her tail lashed the clouds into tatters as she eyed the *Devil's Get*, waiting and watching.

I do not care for this. She growled deep in her belly, like a rumble of thunder.

We must wait or you will fail.

Her tail lashed with more violence, the rumble went deeper. Below her the muffled glow of her emberlings shown like a small sun, beckoning from within. The urge to dive and crack the timbers like an oyster shell nearly overwhelmed her. She gathered herself, muscles tensing and earthfire hardening her scales like the purest iron. The angle of her wings tilted, her body dipped, ready to take the *Devil* down, when Morrow cried out, *No!*

The mental shout disrupted her focus, instantly, brutally, yanking her out of the dive. She shuddered and swayed and nearly roared in challenge. *No! Don't, m'lady!* She felt urgency in Morrow's thoughts. It softened her fury toward him.

You mustn't, Morrow warned her. *Tulo is the key, you must wait until he returns or your emberlings will never be safe. He hunts them like a pig finds truffles, like he has some sense for them. None other that I know of, save the captain and his man, Cragg, have the secret of the runestones, finding them…making them; take those men and that knowledge dies with them. Take the stones and leave them free and you will face a constant battle.*

Camirel continued to circle, tail still thrashing, wings cutting the air until the sea writhed and whitecaps battered the harbor and the ships at dock. Her muzzle twitched as she quietly muttered with impatience.

Finally, a few hours before dawn, two forms swaggered the length of the pier. *It is them,* Morrow whispered into Cami's thoughts. As she descended, she slowly released her hold on the earthfire, her form dwindling as she came lower. Cami felt a mental gasp from Morrow as she thought the runes to hide her from all senses.

You mustn't do that! Not again, never close to him. Frantic images of a gaudy blade and steel collars accompanied Morrow's thoughts as Cami settled to the deck, sliding into the shadows as the pirates stepped onto the gang plank.

Morrow babbled on, thoughts darting erratically, forcing her to winnow through for what was relevant and block out all else. *Speak a rune in his proximity and Tulo will enslave you. The stone in the pommel of his dagger, it is one of your emberlings, spelled to bind runecasters. Speak a rune and the stone flares. If Tulo speaks the trigger word, your thoughts, your body, are bound as if by iron. He will capture us. You will wake with the gleam of a sharp new necklace circling your throat.*

Cursing, Cami instinctively dropped back deeper into the shadows, though the pirates could not sense her even had she stood boldfaced before them. Morrow never shared the details of his ending, but she had seen his remains and the manner of his death. A growl rumbled deep in her belly.

Tulo had stolen her children, abused and twisted them, sought to sell them. He would not escape her wrath. Cami doubted such a thing would have effect on her, but she could not risk the testing of that conviction.

All runes, or just new workings? she asked.

New only. He seeks to bind any runecaster he can, to profit from their skills. Set runes are too common, and do not guarantee those bearing them have an ability for 'casting. Catch too many of that sort and the scheme is revealed.

Satisfaction sharpened Cami's features. Runecasting was the least of her talents. Unlike most of mankind, she was not restricted to runes; her will was enough. What was more, her rebirth linked her directly to the earthfire. She drew on it now. This close to the water — the natural rival to fire — it took an effort, but she increased her will and once more transformed into an armored version of herself, a melding of woman and dragon, armed with talons and teeth, muscle sheathed in scale no man or beast could pierce.

It was unlikely the pirate could even sense the working. Only one person had ever challenged her, before the change or after: the witch, Malizia. More than once that one had sought to steal the emberling Camirel had guarded before she'd even known its secret. Malizia had nearly succeeded. It was because of the witch that the Last Mother was no more. The woman was unnatural and ruthless. Something drove her to eradicate dragonkind from the world; but for the emberlings and Cami herself, she had achieved her goal. Zia's power was peculiar and had no link to the earthfire. She consorted with leviathans, creatures whose power was born of water, the single beast that was a threat to a dragon. Malizia's magic was the only thing Cami had encountered capable of disrupting her own, unless she shielded against it.

Camirel put the woman from her thoughts as she watched Tulo cross the deck, waited boldly by the door to his cabin, knowing it by the presence of the emberlings within. A smirk twitched her lips as he murmured his trigger word to open the portal. The rune was a simple one she could have easily broken, but it would have cost her time and she could not risk being wrong about the dagger spell, linked as it was to an emberling. It took no effort to slip in behind him, though, and to block the counterword meant to lock it tight again.

The man crossed the cabin and sank into a crouch beside an iron-bound chest chuckling in a self-pleased manner. His hand ran over the planks, caressed the iron bands until he swayed slightly and chuckled some more, releasing whisky vapors on each breath. He murmured a word expectantly. Cami could hear the syllables slur, sensed the flaw in the magic even before he cursed and brought a fist down hard on the chest. Gently and unnoticed, she used her mind to steady him. He muttered and twitched as if some part of him sensed her. She wondered at it; he should not have been able to. Tulo shook his head and turned back to the chest before him, betraying no sign that her efforts tripped the binding rune. Cami relaxed and watched closely as the pirate breathed deep and tried again. This time a *click* sounded and the lock fell open.

In the silence of her mind, Morrow gasped. Cami barely noticed as the lid to the chest rose. Her heart cried out and her voice joined it.

That was when she realized something was horribly wrong.

The captain spun about at her cry, his back to the chest and a plain boot dagger in his hand, already casting it before his eyes focused upon her. She hissed and flinched as the blade sank into her shoulder, striking scales that had softened to thick hide. So focused was she on her goal she had not noticed the earthfire dampen.

A wicked, throaty laugh sounded from the cabin door as a curse came to Cami's lips.

"A lovely bonus then, quite unexpected!"

"Malizia," Camirel growled even as the captain called out "Zia!" in a voice both confused and angry. Cami screamed and half spun herself, one hand clutching the hilt of the dagger, as she forced her will through the other in a mage blast meant to shred the witch's focus. The effort was a waste; between the water below and the witch's influence nearby the blast barely set a warm breeze ruffling Malizia's hair, which slowly morphed from an old woman's scraggly grey, to a youthful woman's full, ebon locks.

Even as the witch reverted to her true form, the last of Camirel's scales faded away until she found herself naked, bleeding, and vulnerable before her nemesis. Cami had time only to grip the emberling pouch bound round her waist before the witch's fingers flicked in her direction. In deep contrast to the warmth of Morrow's stone, a chilled stream of magic lashed her, binding Camirel's limbs like the cold grip of the sea's deep currents. To add further insult, Zia then turned away, as if she were of no further consequence.

"Cragg!" The captain bellowed, shocked sober and steady. "Rally the men!"

Malizia laughed again, even more wicked than before, and sent another tendril to bind Tulo. She sauntered forward and brought up her finger to silence his lips. "Best not to disturb the dead, *captain*. They are so unsettled when newly made."

"Witch!" he cried and strained against his unseen bonds.

"Why yes, pity you are only now so observant." She purred and wrapped a single hand around his throat, casually crushing it with all the weight of the ocean below. The expression on her face as she let go was obscene. She stared over her shoulder a moment, catching Cami's eye, and then leaned past Tulo's crumbled corpse to lift a stone from the chest. "A few moments sooner," the witch confided, "and I might have had to work for my treat. This way… easier, perhaps, but less satisfying."

Zia turned until Camirel had clear view of the emerald emberling held aloft.

At that moment, Morrow stirred with the mental equivalent of a caught breath. *The stone she holds…the rune it is etched with is a death curse! Murmur this word…* He spoke the trigger into her mind, but Cami hesitated; would the rune work its magic against the witch or would her shielding block it? Who then would the curse target? Camirel herself? An innocent beyond this vessel? Through the open door she could hear the sounds of the docks coming alive for the day, providing targets aplenty, should the spell fly wild.

Say it! Before she comes. Morrow's thoughts were frantic, as if her safety mattered to him, thought perhaps it did, if only in relation to his own. It didn't matter, really, Cami's indecision already faded, too weak to stand against her vivid memories of past dealings with the witch. There was no doubting the evil Malizia would inflict on the world if left unchecked. Rather than speak aloud, Camirel thought the word as clear and willful as she was able.

Green fire lit the room. The air sizzled and snapped, the sound oddly in harmony with Malizia's screech as the curse hit her. Her body jerked and her fingers, clenched about the stone, shriveled. With a snarl the witch focused her will upon the limb, halting the curse at the wrist before turning her gaze on Camirel. Such fury Cami had never seen, and Morrow's stone trembled against her thigh.

Damn! The failure was bitter, though her fears had been unrealized.

The witch's yellow eyes blazed with the promise of slow retribution and her expression twisted vindictively with glee. But first she pursed her lips and blew a stream of water magic until ice encased both the stone and her hand. Zia brought her wrist down hard on the edge of the chest until both hand and stone shattered. Magic sealed the wound.

The earth cried out through Camirel as the emberling died; grief blistered her throat as hot tears etched her cheeks and with that her link to the earthfire grew a little stronger. The faint echo of talons formed at fingertips that crushed the pouch as her hand fisted protectively over the emberling containing Morrow. The fire in her grew as Malizia lifted another runestone.

"No," Camirel growled low and tight, wrath burning off the chill of her mage bindings. She flexed and felt the flow of scales creep across her flesh closing her own wound. She willed the scales flesh-tone even as she drew harder on the earthfire, linked through the emberling in her grasp and those blazing across the room. She prayed the link stronger, but feared it was not enough to overpower the witch's spell.

Malizia sneered and summoned her water magic, slinked closer and pursed her lips, ready to send a second spell stream to extinguish the young she held in her remaining hand.

Camirel roared and fought her bindings. She could not yet work her magic beyond her form and her arms remained locked, but her body rocked and her eyes narrowed. She waited for the witch to draw near. With the whisper of a breath, she murmured a promise, loud enough for Malizia to hear, but not make out.

Venom in her gaze, the witch moved closer until her face filled Cami's vision. "You are a splinter beneath my nail, *girl*; it will be a pleasure...." Cami rolled her eyes and slammed her head forward, cutting off Zia's prattle. The emberling dropped as the stunned witch crumbled. It landed beside Cami's foot against her flesh. At its touch the earthfire in her flared brighter. She flexed and expanded until the water bonds shattered even as Zia stirred at her feet.

Cami lunged down. Her right hand closed around the emberling first, her left shoved the witch away. They grappled and fought like common wenches, because neither possessing enough control of her magic to summon a strike. As they wrestled around the cabin they heard the sound of footsteps coming up the plank, followed by an outcry as whoever boarded discovered Malizia's misdeeds. Cursing, Camirel thumped the witch's head against the cedar chest, once, and then twice before her opponent lost her one-handed grip on Cami's throat. Shoving the evil woman aside, Camirel lunged for the open chest, grabbing the emberlings and thrusting them into her pouch.

Her magic completely restored, she turned to deal with Malizia. The witch had gained her feet and some command of her own magic. She stood between the Last Mother's champion and the door. Hatred wafted thick in the air, turning it rank and sour.

Camirel felt the weight of realization: One of them would not leave this cabin. She readied her defenses, sank the pouch and its precious content beneath dragon hide, and called forth the lethal power of earthfire. Across from her, Malizia similarly prepared as she summoned the cold, crushing weight of the deep.

Before either could strike, more feet pounded up the gang plank, bearing the growing uproar closer. Cami's gaze darted to the door.

Foolish, but she couldn't help it.

Zia struck. A tsunami of power slammed Camirel into the hull. She lay in the far corner of the cabin, stunned, barely holding on to consciousness, and could do nothing as the earthfire slid from her grip. There came the faint sound of shattering glass and Cami felt the ocean breeze, moist and cool upon her skin. Her eyes fought to focus. She found herself alone, feeling more than hearing the thud of heavy footsteps approach the cabin.

She's gone, m'lady! Morrow said. *You have to get up, you have to get away!*

Cami shushed him, her hand lightly patting his runestone, which she again found herself clutching.

So, Malizia had fled, empty-handed, leaving Camirel to the… mercy…of the authorities. Let the witch enjoy her reprieve. They would meet again; for now, content with the weight of the ember-lings warming her chilled and aching body, Camirel drew enough earthfire to hide herself from all senses, scaled skin reflecting wood tones. *It is well,* she said to Morrow. *Hush, my friend, and stop calling me m'lady. My name is Camirel.* He fell silent and she could feel a subtle change in him, a quiet joy. She lay there, undetected by the authorities, waiting with him in comfortable silence for the uproar to die down.

On "To Reach for Distant Shores"

What is a story but the marriage of vision and voice? In "To Reach For Distant Shores" Danielle Ackley-McPhail blends a vivid and strikingly beautiful dream of a world beyond reach with the unique voice of a denizen of the sea. This is a tale of tragedy, of burning desire, of hope, and ultimately of kindness and a debt repaid. And it is written with an elegance and passion that captures perfectly the twin threads of ambition and sensual fulfillment that drive her point-of-view character. Often we forget that a tale need not be long or filled with violence to be effective. This story is a gem; small, gleaming, multi-faceted. Peer into its depths and be transported.

— David B. Coe / D.B. Jackson,
author of *The Thieftaker Chronicles*

To Reach for Distant Shores

A Tale from the World of the Silver Moon

THE ANSWERS TO MY DREAMS WERE BROUGHT TO ME BY A FLASH storm come up from the south off the sea—violent, sudden, unexpected. The winds rarely drove from that direction, but when they did it was gloriously primal. I could feel them in the fine bones of my body, like the warning my whisker hairs sent when something dangerous loomed close by.

While my sisters and brothers dove down deep at the threat of the storm, I wended my way upward, to peer from the lee of the rocks jutting from the slapping waves, my eyes trained on the water's surface and the skies, avidly watching for the signs that would come swift and sudden and much too late for any about on the surface to heed. In the distance, barely heard, the air rumbled warning of the tempest's approach. With vague interest I noticed narrow, oblong bladders high up in the sky, floating like the jellies beneath the waves, right down to the tendrils dangling from their

core. Tiny trailers of electric static crackled like an eel's warning across the bladder's skin before the energy was gone, dispersed on the quickening wind.

Again my bones shivered as the storm drew ever closer. This was the moment when down close to the water the air fell too still. My eyes scanned the sea, drawn by vibrations on the surface. To my left a large mass drifted by like a rare leviathan risen from the depths in the dark hour to let the light of the unseen moon brush its skin. It was a made thing, a ship, filled with man-things scurrying about at this first hint of the coming storm. As the vessel passed, thunder rumbled faintly in the distance, popping closer and closer. The rapidly darkening clouds lit up and sudden trails of lightning danced down from the sky, colliding with each other and the mass on the water, high up where thin, straight branches rose like webbed fingers to touch the air.

I watched with eager eyes, my breath barely rippling the froth on the waves. My hands gripped tight to the moss-coated rocks as my fins were nibbled clean by the tiny fish living in the shoals, poised to escape beneath the depths when the heavens finally crashed down to whip the waves into a frenzy.

I left my leaving long, clinging in place as the air charged and crackled and thunderclouds of a sudden boiled up on the horizon. With a gleeful laugh, I dove deep and fast just before the stormfront blanketed the world above.

None on water or in air saw mercy from that tempest. I came up to the shallows when the worst passed, eager to see the evidence of the storm's might. With care I darted from mass to mass, just beneath the water. All I found was broken by the punch of the waves and wind, bitten by the power of the lightning. Fragments of those odd conveyances rained down, caught and cradled a moment before being swallowed by the sea.

I turned my attention to the masters of those vessels. The bodies I left for the currents to slurp down, or batter upon the distant sands as they may. There was one I came across with warmth yet in his veins. I wrapped both arms around and drew him down with me. Beneath the runnels of blood and scraggled hair there was something of his face that spoke of fear. He jerked and thrashed as the waves closed overhead, his odd, split tail flailing uselessly against my single powerful one. I murmured reassurances in his ear, but he continued to struggle. Grimacing, I tightened my grip and swam more swiftly to gain us the sanctuary of my private grotto.

I held an eager breath. Never had I had this chance before. To speak to one who made their home above the water. One who knew of the sky jellies. I held little if any doubt of communication between us. In my long life I had travelled far and listened well, I was certain I could speak and understand every language the man-things spoke near the sea — which was to say all of them.

I knew what I would ask him. The only thing I cared to ask him: *How? How do you reach the sky?* It was my dearest dream to take my place up there, to gain those distant shores and swim the waters of the unseen moon. I dreamt of dancing with the lightning, of climbing its jagged bolts into the heavens. There were oceans there. I could not see them, but I could feel their call in the shivers down my scales and the tremors through my whisker hairs. I had no doubt those waters were there. After all, look how much spray rained down to mingle here below.

The lightning climbed up into the sky. Those like the one wrapped in my arms rode the winds. Perhaps the air-jellies were the key to gaining the clouds. This one held the secret. He *would* give it up. My egg sibs scoffed, but I would not rest until I was as cradled by those waters above as I was by my own sea.

And here was my chance to discover the secret to making this so.

But my effort was for naught. By the time we shook off the water's clinging, and I drew the stranger from above up upon my own hidden sands deep below, the warmth had fled him. I stared at his peculiar face and my teeth gnashed, jagged edge against jagged edge. I traced the plump curve of his now-blue lips and peered into strange, near-flat eyes, gone blood-shot and lifeless, as if my answers were written there. They were not. But something did glitter slightly lower. I reached out, pushing aside the odd flaps that covered his chest like a skin torn loose and let flop to either side. Beneath was a wonder. It was an object like lightning-struck sand only smooth and straight and clear. Something encapsulated within glowed faintly. I lifted the thing away, breaking the thin strap it hung from around the dead one's neck. And none too soon.

A splash behind me betrayed an intrusion. "Your bottom-feeder tendencies are showing, my dear."

Phin. Like a case of scale rot, that one had plagued me ever since we were fingerlings. Even in the sac he was rotten, I was sure. Someday, when I spawned my young, I would eat any eggs that held darkness such as his, for Phin had one goal: by word and deed, inflict what harm he may and often. His disdainful tone sent my lips into a snarl. As if I would feed upon a thinking being.

Before he spied it, I slipped my prize into the kelp bands I'd strung about my waist for carrying such things as I did not wish to hold in my hands. I then turned and glared at where he lounged, flukes in the water, arms on the sands, bracing him up. As ever, his eyes were mocking.

He could not have noticed my expression.

Not when he was too busy staring up and down the length of me, eyes lingering in the region of my pelvic fins. Hissing with annoyance and distaste, I heaved the strange one to my shoulder. With a wiggle of my fins and tail I shoved past my egg brother — we were sheltered in the same nest, though not spawned from the same source — before sliding into the water, hauling the corpse to the grotto entrance where I let the eager current reclaim its prize.

Unburdened but still weighed down, I undulated upward. The surface was choppy yet, dotted with flotsam not claimed by the depths, but the clouds had vanished as quickly as they'd come, leaving the sky deep and dark and finely speckled like a dolphin.

I let my head fall back, eyes closed, and breathed deep of the cleansed, ozone-scented air, savoring the lingering taste of salt water tinged with fresh-churned kelp on my lips. Slowly my muscles unbunched. My eyes opened to scan the sky. To the left, high up, I spied a patch seemingly void of stars. A dark cloud? One of the sky jellies? I could not say, but without a doubt I could dream. With a few powerful strokes of my tail I swam again toward the rocks, hauled myself up and let the moonbeams caress my skin and scales. I looked up to the larger moon, the one all could see. Its touch was cool, soft. Pleasant, but nothing more. The other…the hidden moon…I glowed with the charge it imbued. Warmth bathed me on the inside, despite the chill of the night.

Someday….Someday I would gain that vaunted moon's shores and swim in its vibrant seas.

Forcing my gaze down and away lest I remain mesmerized for longer than was safe, I looked to the object tucked within my kelp bands. My hand trembled as I drew it out with care. It was fine, more delicate than I would have thought possible. I could imagine neither its purpose nor manner of creation. I had taken it because it caught my eye. I kept it for it seemed a treasure, something of value to the lost soul I had claimed it from. Perhaps it would serve a purpose for me, as lure or boon to one from his world who might aid me. I secured it once more, not wanting the jealous waves to claim my prize.

That was when I heard it. A broken sound. A weak one. It was foreign even to me, who had ventured forth through all the earthly seas available to me — which was to say, all of them. I was a powerful swimmer.

My dorsal fronds stiffened, not quite billowing as they would beneath the waves, but nonetheless they snapped at the air in eager anticipation. This was a new thing. I angled my head to capture the sound. To pinpoint the source. It had something of a seal's bark — were the seal half dead. And something of the seagull's caw, only much less demanding. I could not for a moment imagine what made such a sound. Taut with the need to know, I drew myself across the rocks, up through the crevice that split this oceanic outcrop. I was silent as I moved, the muscles in my tail bunching to push against the rock, aiding my arms as they may. As I drew closer to the sound I slowed my motions. A tall, thin spire of rock jutted high overhead. With care, I placed my webbed fingers against its jagged mass and pulled myself up to peer around the bulk of it.

The water glittered in the moonlight as it could not hope to beneath the sun, else I would not have noticed. An odd form clinging to the base of the outcrop, half in and half out of the waves, broke up that liquid shimmer. It humped first large, then smaller, holding to the rocks as tight as a barnacle did. There was the odd glimmer as the moon stroked something wet and sleek, but only in patches, as if the form were not all of one thing.

I almost lost my grip and tumbled down as suddenly a different, higher wail rose, piercing my delicate ears clear through. And then I saw the one form was two, small huddled against the large. My pelvic fins fluttered instinctually. I watched as the bigger of the two pulled the other close to shelter against her…for her it was, I could see as the moon now caressed the paleness of her face. The little one looked up and a sound escaped me. It was a boy-thing, small lips full and flat eyes familiar, though lacking the tinge of blood red last seen upon the eyes of another face. Were the sea kinder, I could see this one might grow into the man-thing I'd gripped in my arms not long ago.

Perhaps it was my earlier thoughts of spawning, but an ache settled in my chest to see that young one at the mercy of the sea. I leaned closer, my head tilted for a better view, my ear hole bent toward them to pick up the words drifting on the night's breeze.

"He said that he would find us…he promised. If anything happened to the ship," the woman-thing murmured through cracked lips. Her words drifted, broken and as faint as the sounds she'd first made. "Find a place of safety, he said and signal him.

He will come. He promised. But the flare…it's gone." Her one hand rose briefly to touch an object around her neck. From a familiar strap hung the fragments of what seemed the cousin to the object hidden in my kelp bands. As the woman-thing slid deeper in the water she scrambled to cling to the rocks once more.

More of the tortured sounds, point and counterpoint, high voice and low. Though the sounds hurt my ears I remained perched in my crevice, oddly captivated by the scene below. As I stayed there, the night air brushed over my form, gentle but persistent, until my skin and scales itched and twitched and tightened enough to bring me to wailing myself. The depths called to me, soothing and wet, cool and dark, and yet I watched until I spied the boy-thing slide into the grip of the waves. The woman-thing cried out and dove fearlessly after, in several long moments surfacing with her sputtering young. He choked and gasped as I have never heard a creature come from the sea. Great wracking coughs spewed water upon the rocks. My gaze went to his neck. I gasped myself and my gills twitched in empathy when realization dawned: as the fish remained ever below, these man-things thrived only above. My mouth gaped with remorse as my eyes opened to what I had done in drawing the man-thing down beneath the waves. I had borne no malice, yet like Phin I'd wreaked great harm. Even could I wrest the man-thing from the sea the deed could not be undone. He would not breathe again, nor return to these steadfastly waiting. But there was one thing I could do in restitution. My numb fingers slid down to grip the rod still lodged within my now-dry kelp bands. It had clearly held import for him, kept, as it was, hidden against his breast. I suspect this was another of the flares the woman-thing worried over.

I knew what I must do.

Sliding back down the outcrop, harsh rock scraping free dried scales as I went, I slipped with a grateful sigh back into the sea. Powerful twitches of my tail sent me around the rocks to where the two I'd watched still clung. From this new vantage point I saw they perched because they could not climb higher against the algae-coated rock. This I could fix. The night air splintered with their shrieks as I braced against their bottoms, first the boy-thing, then the woman-thing, and with powerful thrusts of my tail surged forward, propelling them from the sea and up onto the rocks. They scrambled higher, clutching each other in as tight a grip as I'd held their man-thing when I drew him under the sea. I bobbed there where they had clung, merely watching, bemused but content that the waters would not have them. I met the gaze of the woman-thing, remorse in my eyes, though my tongue remained silent.

I had not the words to make my deed right, none to excuse them. I bowed my head down as I slid my hand into the kelp band, working the object free. It glowed in the moonlight as I brought it forth and the terror in the woman-thing's expression lightened with a gleam of hope. Like a crab, she sidled toward my outstretched hand, snatching my prize and scurrying back.

Without a word I turned away and dropped beneath the waves, but not before I glanced a fleeting moment up into the sky. Someday I would dance with the lightning, and climb its jagged bolts into the heavens. Someday…I would reach those distant shores to swim the seas of the unseen moon.

But not today.

Sweet Liam Roanes

You left behind a trail
…footprints in the sands
…ripples through the waves
…blissful agony etched upon my heart
Leading me to the precipice.

Your calls were a siren song
…drifting on the wind,
…rising from the surf
…echoing in my cries,
Tempting me at the cliff's edge.

Lost in the memory of your skin
…like cream silk against my lips
…like slick grey velvet beneath my fingertips
…like salty sweetness tipping my tongue
Drawing me into your madness.

Why I did not notice
The melancholy edge to your laughter
…the sorrow underlying the joy
in your endless eyes?

Blessed of the divine children
Cursed immortal soul
Call down a storm upon this shore
That nature may cry my tears

For I have lost my heart to a selkie,
And I've lost my selkie to the sea.

Consigned to the Sea

"Blessed of the Divine Children
Cursed Immortal Soul
Call down a storm upon these shores
That nature may cry my tears."

—Excerpt from *Sweet Liam Roanes*

SEVEN TEARS FELL INTO THE SEA.

They spread my sorrow among the foam and surf, mingled it with the waves until it was destined to touch every shore upon the earth ere the water's wandering was done.

One tear for every year gone by since my husband went his way.

Seven tears fell into the sea.

'Tis said we all return to whence we began; why shouldn't they?

It was high tide. The ship that bore me away recklessly hugged the rocky coast off the Orkneys. At my back I heard a thudding tread, familiar and hated, measuring the length of the weathered deck, owning it. Louder with each step, closer with each tear. The rest turned to hot ash in my eyes as the devil drew near.

"Well, have you decided, poppet?"

I remained turned away and silent, my back stiff and straight and indignant. Captain Darian Gow merely laughed and wrenched me around; his large, thick fingers bruised my bare shoulder, his hard, shadowed jaw lowered inches from my face.

"Have. You. Decided?" His words were measured and deadly calm. Overhead, terns cried a strident warning as they hovered just past the rigging. Below, waves pounded the hull in a siege as old as seafaring ways. My voice rebelled against any answer.

I stood before him with my back pressed hard against the rail, shivering despite the sun, in a dress of crimson crushed velvet he'd flung at me earlier, replacement for the widow's weeds they'd torn from my body before they'd even brought me aboard. It was a whore's dress. Quite literally, in fact, I had no doubt. Blood rubies and rare black seed pearls crusted what bodice there was and the black-satin-lined skirts were indecently slit, fore and aft. A costly whore's dress, but one just the same. I'd been given no petticoats to serve my modesty.

Anger mingled with the fear in my heart. I smothered it for a time with slow, even breaths. I tried one final bid, begging freedom for my daughter. "Will ye na set her safe upon Eynhallow? An ye do, I'll gladly shew ye the way ye seek."

Captain Gow straightened. His eyelids lowered half-mast and his mouth curved but a degree at one corner. He looked back at the crew on the deck and in the rigging. He looked forward and pointedly scanned the shore as if the route he sought would magically appear to him; we both knew he had no hope of hiding his ship among the Islands to evade the King's Navy without a native such as myself to guide him along the safe paths. Finally, he leaned forward once more, the other corner of his mouth joining the first, as if he were amused.

I lifted my own chin and forced myself to ignore his massive hands settling on the hilts of his cutlass and saber. No expression at all did I allow upon my face.

He laughed as if delighted and came even closer by my ear.

"What a pretty package you make in my gift," he said, his breath stirring the fine ebon locks curled around my ear while the wind tugged at the rest of the tresses forcefully unbound at my capture. "You're lucky for the decency of even that dress, you know..." He turned away to swagger toward the stern, calling out over his shoulder when he was far enough amidships for his voice to carry to both myself and the crew. "Your bonnie lass...she has none."

Lust glimmered in every eye I could see, and none of it directed toward me. My gut clenched and my pulse tripped faster. I was driven by the need to rush for the hold where they'd imprisoned my daughter, but I knew I would not be let near. I gasped and clutched the rail until a nail tore. The pain of my finger kept me anchored firm against my instinct. I remained still, the cold flow of air off the North Sea chilled me, while the fires of hell licked at my thoughts, sparked by his implicit threat. I could not hold back the growl as fury crept over my fear, burying it. The vile Gow heard. Heard and laughed once more.

"I've the charts laid out in my cabin, woman, if that will help you get your bearing."

I trembled such that the satin lining of the dress brushed my bare flesh in an obscene caress. My teeth clenched and every muscle flinched away from the sensation until I was a hard, tight effigy of myself. I spun around to stare out at the sea, battling both rage and despair. I closed my burning eyes and lifted my face to the constant breeze, letting it dry those tears that escaped the confines of my lashes. The wind whipping about me murmured empty comfort. Mingled with its fickle whisper I heard a call that haunted both my waking hours and my sleep. My fingers locked upon the rail and my body strained. To hear...to leap...I could not say.

The wind carried but the sounds of surf and gulls. I eyed the rocky islets and the choppy wake. Nowhere did I spy a trace of life not on the wing. Had I imagined that familiar call?

Hope bled away.

I turned my back upon the lure of the waves. The final freedom I could not claim. I worked my way across the ship toward the hold, deftly evading the crew as they bustled about the deck, keeping my gaze turned from those clambering like monkeys among the rigging. They ogled, they cast lewd comments, but they dared not touch. The dress I wore...the captain's mark upon me, sure as if he'd scrawled his name across my near-bare breast.

Heedless of that self-same dress, when I reached the hold I crouched upon the deck as if weary, pooling the hated skirts among the brine and slime cast up by the sea. None shouted me away; none laid their rough hands upon me. My head drooped forward to rest against the grate. I whistled a soft trill distinctly out of place upon the sea.

Scurrying sounded below, followed by the slight thud of something — a hogshead or a crate — banging against the hull timbers as my child hauled herself atop them. I peered down through false twilight, my face shielded from the pirates' sight by the tangled mass of my unbound curls. My daughter stared back. Her eyes — as dark and soulful as any seal cub's — met mine, large and glimmering and fearful. Her naked flesh shone pallid against the darkness; a sickly blue-white, as if she'd already been claimed by the sea.

A sob escaped me, and I lurched up, my slender arm thrust down through the gap.

"Mam!" Kate cried, both joyous and pleading. She reached for me, heedless of her precarious perch, stretching up until our fingers twined.

The deck creaked behind me. I barely heard. Why my arm did not snap, I do not know, but I tasted blood upon my lips as I jerked back from the jarring smack delivered by Captain Gow's hand. From below I heard my daughter yelp with pain as my torn nail caught at the delicate tissue of her webbed hand.

"The charts are in my cabin." His voice rumbled like the threat of thunder. "Not the hold. If I spy you near it again before you've shown me the course, you'll watch your whelp go to the crew."

Rage overcame my common sense.

"Ye devil! Ye bastard! Ye unwashed cock of a disease-ridden popinjay!" I hurled my fists as swiftly as my curses. My nails drew blood and my bare feet bruised themselves against his hard-muscled legs. So focused was my fury, I barely felt the hands of the first mate, McCray, as he pulled me off and restrained me.

The crew went still and silent. The air itself drew taut, and even the terns held their cries.

"Stand away from her," Gow ordered in a low, flat tone.

My eyes widened as sense came back to me. I trembled and hid my hands, scarcely believing what I'd done, though I could see the bloody welts that marred the captain's cheek. I opened my mouth to beg mercy for my daughter, but closed it without a word spoken. I dare not remind him he could strike me most fatally through her.

His arm lashed out once more, as swift and hard as a boom coming about on a schooner. I felt blood fly from my temple as I landed across the deck inches from a long drop and a watery death.

All traces of warmth left my body. Fear went the way of hope and darkness crept into the void. I fought that darkness off, waiting for rough hands to seize me, praying I would not hear the hold hatch lifted and my daughter pay for my folly. Only the muffled sound of the crew resuming their duties slipped past the ringing in my ears. As if from far off, I felt the boards tremble as Captain Gow strode away.

They left me there.

I dared not believe it. It was a struggle, but I raised my head. The effort was wasted: my eyes showed me naught but the blurred colors of the sea. I closed them again and surrendered to the darkness.

Twilight fog wreathed the ship ere I woke again. I heard the murmur of the men on watch, though I could not see them. My body ached and the mist-dampened velvet weighed me like an anchor. What purpose to rise? I did not bother, simply letting myself drift, staring at that little patch of sea before me. If not for Kate I might have crawled those last inches, cast myself into that final freedom I'd earlier refused. But I would not leave her to them by any choice of my own.

A noise drew me from the stupor: The sharp, sudden sound of something breaking the skin of the water. I edged closer to the railless gap meant for the gang plank. The sea appeared like a liquid jewel before me, rippling and flowing, all but where it sprouted a cluster of long, graceful whiskers. Raised just above the surface of the water, thick-fringed, black glossy eyes met my own. Did I imagine the anguish they held? Did I imagine a familiar glint? I strained my yet-blurred gaze looking for a collar of dapple spots strung like pearls about the seal's neck, but it was impossible to see.

It did not matter. I knew even if this were not he, my charge would still reach him.

"A storm," I hissed to the creature. "A storm, Liam Roanes, ten -thousand times as fierce as those ye've sent me before an' I'll ne'er curse yer name again!"

Naught but a lightening of the mists proclaimed the dawn, that and the calls of the crew going about the day's duties. My opening eyes burned, but they focused. I saw quite clearly the grey boards of the deck streaked red-black by my blood. I shifted myself — as much to avoid the sight as to determine that I could — and barely swallowed a groan as I did so. My stomach heaved and the ship seemed to tilt beneath me. Everywhere I ached, but I could not remain here. Slowly I fought off weakness and worked my way to my knees. The salty air stung my battered flesh and I swayed as my muscles rebelled. As I struggled to rise further, something disturbed the air behind me.

"Ah, perfect." Gow's mocking word drifted to my ears as a hard-bristled brush crashed down upon my fingers leaving the skin scored. "You can clean up your mess while you are so suitably poised. In fact, the whole deck could use a scrubbing.

"McCray," he called across the ship, "bring our lovely a pail and see she scrubs from aft to stern."

I could not help but flinch as a bucket of foul water landed before me. Half the content slopped out, soaking the front of my dress, molding it even more — if possible — to my body. I could feel both of them stare.

"When you're done, come to my cabin. I'll have the charts waiting for you." The captain paused a moment and a shiver ran from my neck to my toes. "And when I have my heading, we'll see about...cleaning...that dress."

My body trembled with fatigue as I dropped the brush into the bucket for the last time. Above, the weak sun crested the noon hour. The morning's efforts left my fingers cracked and bleeding, but no bit of blood or brine or salt marred the deck. The same could not be said for my dress. I sighed and slumped against the nearest crate, head lolling forward. My dull eyes drifted closed but a moment.

"To your feet, you lazy wench!"

I opened my eyes and slowly rolled my head back. Captain Gow stood over me, his expression as dark and dangerous as the depths of the sea. Weary and ill, I could not care. I'd no strength left in me to comply. His lips snarled as I remain where I was. His hand whipped out to grasp my arm. With no effort at all he hauled me up and whirled me against him.

I groaned and my stomach heaved once more, though it held naught.

The captain held me at the length of his arm and shook. "My patience is no more, wench! You were ordered to my cabin. I will have the heading. Now! Or be it on your soul the hell visited upon you and your brat...our ship holds a full complement, the end will be a long time coming."

My heart threatened to stop and were I not weak with injury and exhaustion, I know not which I would have done: fall upon my knees and beg him to spare my Katie, or summon my rage and again cast myself at him until all his face were bloody.

The crew turned their eyes upon us at Gow's threat. I sensed their anticipation and smelled the rank odor of their lust. I drew myself up straight, my gaze sharpening. I made no effort to hide my hatred. I jerked my arm away and the captain let me; surely, only because it humored him. My dignity was a thin shell closed about me. Inside, my heart screamed. Screamed in fear and rage and bloodlust. That this man would treat us so, that he would threaten us and go unpunished. Worse yet, I had no doubt, whether I did as he bade me or not, in the end our fates would be the same. *A storm, Liam, now!* my soul whispered, low and lethal. *Now, if you had ever a care for your daughter!*

A bark, deep and menacing, sounded off the port bow, from the rocky shore not half a league ahead of us.

I darted my eyes in that direction and spied a massive bull seal with dark spots about his throat in sharp contrast to his light brown pelt. He was as slick as wet velvet from the sea. His pose both regal and aggressive. I imagined, could I see them, his eyes would be dark and hard as coal.

Tension poured away from me, leaving me limp with relief. I had to dip my head to shield the slight curve of my smile from the captain's gaze. I heard hundreds of seals break the surface of the water, the slap as they hauled sleek, wet muscle upon the spray-drenched rocks. In moments, a mighty chorus welled up.

A sob popped upon my lips at the sound of answered prayer. Fear still tightened the flesh about my eyes at the thought of my daughter deep in the hold, but I forced it away. I had to have faith she would be free before long.

The tone of the selkie-song shifted and changed, deepening as it crashed harshly upon all our ears. In moments, the waters surrounding us went still as glass. Every bird winged away without even a cry. Far off, the clouds rumbled. The sound rolled closer and the grey sky took on an ominous yellowish tinge. Pirates cursed, their motions jerky and ill at ease. One in the rigging drew his pistol. There was a sharp click as the man cocked the weapon and took aim at the shore, though nothing short of maybe the cannons had that range.

"They're only beasts. Put up your weapon, you fool," Gow said, a tick at his jaw betraying his own doubt. "Secure the vessel for a squall." The men scrambled to comply. He then turned his eye upon me. "The course, woman, before we're caught in the blow."

I locked my gaze on Liam. He gave a short, sharp bark and a toss of his bewhiskered head toward the mouth of a nearby inlet. It was most decidedly not the one Gow sought. Bobbing in agitation, Liam made the same motion again, followed by a prolonged roar. My eyes drifted closed and I gave a single nod.

Gow's fingers tightened upon my arm.

"There," I whimpered the lie, my hand waving limply in the direction Liam bid me. "There is the way ye seek."

The inlet seemed broad and open, but hidden halfway through the passage, deep enough below the choppy waves there was no sign, lay treacherous rocks guaranteed to stove in any hull, no matter how shallow the draft. Combined with the coming storm, the ship and all aboard were doomed.

Better the embrace of the sea, I thought, *than the arms of the sailors.* In my heart, though, I prayed all the while that Liam would at least see his daughter safely to shore. I held no hope for his kindness toward me, not when my love—nor even my favors—had not been enough to hold him by my side.

With a triumphant laugh, Gow jerked me even more tightly against him and crashed his mouth down upon mine. His thick, foul tongue pierced my lips like a dagger before he shoved me away and hurried to the helm.

Trembling and nauseated, I slumped to the deck and crawled toward the hold, unnoticed among the frantic activity as the men altered the ship's course and the vessel made fast. "Katie-Bug," I murmured through the grate, this time not daring to slip my arm through the gap as the increased chop of the waves made the ship buck and bob on the water. "Sweetling?" I cried just a touch louder when my daughter answered not. My heart gave a hard jolt as silence held sway. Then, from just below me, high up near the hatch, a pale flutter; my daughter's hand, not quite reaching the edge.

I scuttled to the far side, moving with care around barrels and coils of rope thicker than my thigh. I peered into the hold. Eyes as dark and stormy as her father's met mine. Her small, soft-edged jaw was hard set and thrust out, her body taut with waiting. My Kate, as ever attuned to the sea, had climbed up into the bracings and wedged herself into the cradle of the timbers. She'd lashed herself with a coil of rope in a loose knot. One tug upon the end line in either direction and she could tighten herself in place against any storm swell, or set herself free. Pride kindled within me nearly enough to overshadow my fear. I nodded and moved away, not wanting our captors to notice her precautions and wonder why.

"Come about, hard to port!" the captain called out, as I slid myself beneath the steps to the forecastle and braced for what was to come. In our wake, I heard the selkies slide into the sea.

As we sailed down the inlet, the inexperienced aboard cheered at having outrun the storm. The old salts, however, remained tense and edgy. Eyes flickered at the choppy water and back to the shore. Some crossed themselves; others rubbed at tokens they'd attached some superstition to. I prayed to God.

Just before we reached the hidden shoals, hundreds of whiskered faces lifted from the waves. Not one common seal counted among their number now. In the distance, more selkies climbed from the sea to populate the rocks and islets we passed. Some retained their true form; others shed their skins and rose as men and women, unashamedly bare. They ringed the ship.

The crew paled. They moaned. The captain cursed. I held still and fast to the timbers of the stair, as with one voice, the selkies' invocation drowned out the mortal cries.

In the length of a breath, the sky went black as soot. The sea reared up and slammed the ship forward. It crashed down against the rocks hidden by the swells. The sound of timbers giving way below was like a brutal hand wrapped around my throat, depriving me of breath. How long before the ship flooded high enough to reach my daughter's perch? Already we'd taken on enough water that buoyancy was lost. The winds grabbed hold of the vessel, tipped it and shook it, casting several of the men into the sea before once more thrusting the ship hard against the submerged rocks. There we stayed, foundered upon the shoal, listing slightly to starboard.

Katie had been on the starboard side of the hold.

The echo of men's screams filled my ears, and the serenade rising from the surrounding rocks morphed from rousing and tumultuous to sensual and beckoning. Every sound melded masterfully: seal-like barks, the percussive slap of flippers upon the rocks, the rage of the storm, the shriek of tortured timbers, all sounding in dark harmony to the ethereal song lifting like a funnel about the ship. Even the jagged sound of my breath wove its' way into the melody. What a compelling orchestration. It loosened my grip...tempted my will until I had to bite my lip to break the magic's hold, to remain steadfast. I was no unwitting fool, and yet even I nearly succumbed to the siren song.

I clung like a barnacle to my haven below the stairs and watched as my captors cast themselves into the sea. Some dashed upon the rocks until the foam frothed pink-tinged. Others hit the water and found themselves wrapped in welcoming embraces. Fae arms or flippers caressed the pirates' numbing limbs, locking them fast, as they spiraled down beneath the waves. Not even bubbles revealed their final resting place.

The sea was welcome to them...but not to me and mine. We were free of the pirates, now we'd only to escape the ship and the storm. My gaze darted toward the hold. With the hull breached I had to get Katie out before it flooded completely. We were not yet in danger of sinking, thanks to the shoal that held the ship fast, but the storm grew fierce and the vessel would be torn apart before long. Katie and I must get away before the waves were too much for the longboat. Crawling from beneath the risers, I turned toward the hatch.

Shivers wracked my body as waves cresting the side drenched me. The deck shook as the sea pounded against the hull timbers. I fought my way, crawling against the pitch of the deck when I could not keep my feet. Catching up the hook, as I had seen the pirates do, I braced myself against the deck and hauled upon the hatch covering the hold. My muscles cramped and my flesh burned against the friction of unyielding iron. Kate's cries rose like the mewing of a cub; an answering sob raged from my throat. My lips twisted with the strain and yet the grate remained cradled in its mooring. I screamed, cast the hook aside, and wound my fingers around the grate itself, unleashing my fury.

"Had I a full crew each as determined as you, no ship on the sea would stand against us." Laughter danced through the shouted words, but no mirth.

I whirled to catch up the hook once more, only to find it moved from where I'd dropped it. My gaze turned toward the helm. I'd known at the voice what I would see, and still the sight of Captain Gow lounging against the rail, the hook beside him, filled me with hatred more bitter than yarrow. I turned from him, scrambling across the hatch in the hope of finding another weapon to hand. Again, the dress weighted me down. If I saw another day I would burn the hated thing. I was not even halfway across to the other side when the devil hauled me back, his hand locked about my ankle.

Not one to go easy to my death, I grabbed at the hatch, my arms snaking through the gaps. The smell of salt and pitch and fear rose thick about me. Lashing out with my free leg, despite the water-soaked skirts, I caught Gow hard across the jaw. He growled and wrenched me fiercely until I felt the hatch lift from its grooves. I sent a prayer up to God and hugged the hatch tighter. I'd barely been able to lift it on my own, yet the strength of the captain it could not resist. Though my arms screamed with the strain, the hatch came up enough to cant sideways, no longer hardfast over the hold. When, with the next pull, it threatened to come up high enough to crush me, I let loose as it settled once more. With a quick tug, Gow pulled me flush against him.

"Tone deaf, poppet, I am tone deaf," he whispered in my ear, his voice a still and ominous counterpoint to the fury of the storm. "All of this..." he gestured to the continued song of the selkies, "naught but noise." His gaze assessed my body with offensive frankness. "But I imagine your screams will be music to my ears." He wrapped his fingers in my hair, jerking my head back until both neck and spine arched. My eyes rolled, but I forced myself to remain silent. No scream, no gasp, not even the sigh of a breath left my lips, as I watched him draw a dagger. His eyes alight with malice, he ran the point lightly along my cheek, and down my throat, a tickling touch a thousand times worse than the bite of the blade would have been. With the tip, he circled my breast above my heart and pressed just the slightest. I had seen the blade before, and knew its size. Yet it felt like no more than a pinprick piercing my skin. I was all the more chilled by that, as a spot of warmth welled from the wound. It trickled down along my neck until the salty sweet scent nigh overwhelmed me. My mouth gaped silently and I felt my eyes widen to the whites as I waited for Gow to sheath the full length through my heart.

He laughed nastily and stowed the knife. With a hard shove, he pushed me toward starboard. I stumbled and slid down the slick deck, nearly ended up over the side, but for the faithful rail I caught myself upon. I looked over the edge at the oddly canted longboat, before turning to look back at my captor.

"Yer mad an ye expect I'll leave my daughter."

"Have you a choice, faerie's whore?"

"Faerie's *wife*," I snarled, for though forsaken, still I remained. "An nae better a man than he, certainly not the devil Gow."

"Aye, and God and Man sanctioned that marriage, did they?" He sneered back. "And that would be why you and your abomination lived alone on that cursed rock we found you on? Even your faerie didn't want you, let alone good, decent folk."

As the words left his mouth, my hands flexed and fisted. I felt myself growl, though I could not hear it. At the look of contempt upon his face, my rage broke loose of my control. I hurled myself at the man. He waited until I was close, then his leather-clad foot came up to knock aside my legs, sending me to the deck at his feet. Then, gentle as a feather flutters down, he placed his foot upon my throat.

"A quick death I could give you, but you do not deserve it. You've cost me all but my life." His expression roiled dark and dangerous. "I think you must suffer long for all of that." With those words, his eyes slid toward the hold. An ugly little smile crept across his lips. I snarled and bucked, my hands clawing at his ankle. I had no hope against the thick leather of his boots, though, and most definitely not against the weight of him. A little harder he pressed down and the fight in me was, for the moment, done.

Before darkness could completely claim me, there came a thud from across the deck. Gow's head snapped round and his foot came down harder still. I bit back a gasp as a solitary twilight filled my vision.

A curse seemed to reach me from a distance and the weight left my throat. I gulped the air, though it pained me. The twilight receded, leaving in its place a pounding ache. With care, I tilted my head to discover Gow at the ready, his saber in one hand and the other hidden in the folds of his coat. I tried to make out what he held but the folds were too full. Easing back, I peered past him, looking to port.

A bonny sight I beheld: Liam Roanes, in human form, crested the rail, his sealskin draped about his shoulders. I could feel his eyes upon me, large and dark and nary a white to be seen. When he spied my condition his jaw turned to granite. Then Katie cried out from below, and he roared with the voice of an enraged bull seal.

"Ah, come for your *wife*, have you?" Gow said, twisting the word in the same manner he'd said whore before. "Or perhaps your whelp? I'm afraid either way, you've come for naught."

I backed away from Gow and scrambled to my feet, clearing the way for Liam to charge. All the while, I eyed the hook still caught on the helm railing; longed for it such that I could feel its heavy weight in my grasp. Was the captain distracted enough that I could claim it?

My love shrugged off his fur cloak till it pooled on the deck, baring muscles more impressive than even Gow's. "I suggest you try your luck with the sea," Liam said, his voice dangerously even, though his eyes crackled and blazed. "It'll offer you more of a chance than you stand with me."

"So you say, faerie...care to test your words against my steel?"

Gow tossed his saber at Liam, like a spear, in a reckless move I would not have understood were I not close behind him. I watched with dread as his hidden hand shifted. His finger curled and a sharp, familiar click reached my ears. My movement was swift for I had no care for silence or secrecy. As I dove for the hook, the captain pivoted toward me. Before he could come completely about, I wrapped my fingers around the length of iron. He brought his pistol from its hiding place.

I did not wait to see where he would take aim. The weapon belched smoke and I felt a burn along my side that left me cold. Letting loose a bellow, I swung for his head. The ship shivered and lurched, and Gow ducked aside. I staggered against the mast and whirled back around to come at him again. He tossed aside his spent pistol and drew his cutlass. The blade cut the air above my head, bit into timber, and caught fast. I scrambled away from the captain's reach as he wrenched the weapon free. Beneath me, the deck bucked and sheets of rain kept the boards slick. I came up against the rail close by the hoist holding the longboat aloft. Braced, I pivoted and brought my hook arcing up with all my strength just as the captain lunged. His cutlass sliced through the rope securing the longboat as he lashed down at me. The boat crashed into the waves as my weapon connected with Gow's head.

The hook met a spongy resistance that swiftly gave away with a pop, accompanied by a hot salty spray across my face and bosom. I gasped, my stomach heaving. Gow shrieked, and wrenched my weapon from my hands. He staggered back, clutching at the curved length of iron imbedded deep in his eye. One step he took forward, and then another, before crumbling against me, tumbling us both down. The weight of him pinned me to the deck.

Numbly, I shoved him at him to no avail. With a keen, I pushed harder until I could drag myself from beneath him and scramble to my feet. I trembled, scrubbing my hands hard across the wet velvet of my dress, flinching as my fingers brushed too near my side. My hands came away more red than before, yet I felt little at the sight. Instead, images of my love, and Katie, and the past two days billowed through my thoughts, dampening the horror in me. Still, my gaze locked upon the man whose death I had dealt and I could not draw it away. The only thought I had was that the longboat was gone, and with it our slender hope of reaching land.

"Mam!"

My daughter's cry called me back from hell's edge. I shoved all thought of my deed to the recesses of my mind and turned toward the hatch, stumbling as the ache at my side grew sharper. I pushed the pain aside; I had no time for it. Liam no longer stood across the deck, though his sealskin was a rich, dark pool on the timbers. I staggered toward the hold, peering desperately at the nook where Katie had secured herself. Eyes dark and deep and unreadable met mine...another set, near identical but for the size and the uncertainty they held, stared up from just above the water. The level rose as I watched.

"A blade, Sionna...*now*."

Hardly the words of one lovelorn, I thought without bitterness. He had come for his daughter. 'Twas all I had hoped for before he had even appeared. And still despair took a tighter hold upon my heart. I forced it away as my mind conceived the reason for his demand. The rope that bound Katie would have swelled in the immersion, the knot locked tight. I turned without a word and dropped to the deck, my side screaming as I looked for the cutlass Gow had dropped. I was near tears when I could not find it.

Swallowing hard I turned toward the captain's corpse. Remembered with cold clarity the moments before Liam boarded the ship. I did not even flinch as I dove upon the body and shoved it over. Fresh blood marred my hands and face, my dress, but the dagger was clear. I snatched it from its sheath and rushed back to the hold.

Another selkie had appeared. Male or female, I could not tell, though it also was in human form. Its face was too young for the features to betray its gender. It must have come through the gash in the hull. I handed down the blade and watched as Liam slid it between the timber and the line. With one hard jerk, he severed Katie's bonds and thrust the blade back into my hands.

Not knowing her father's face, Katie clung where she was, though the water lapped about her lips. I watched as Liam's expression softened and his eyes glowed like rich onyx. With a closed smile that did not bare his seal's teeth, my husband reached beneath the water for Katie's hand. She jerked back, but he remained as firm as he was gentle. He pulled her hand toward him into the light. Holding his own so they were palm to palm, he spread both their fingers wide. Upon seeing her webbing mirrored by his, all fear and doubt fled Katie's face. Her smile beamed like sunshine upon the snow as she propelled herself out of the water and latched about his neck. I heard the echo of a seal's bark in Liam's laugh and savored the sweet pain of the memories it resurrected.

A smile lit my face as father and daughter at last met. It quickly fled as I watched Liam lower his face, pressing his lips upon Katie's. I saw her cheeks stretch as he forced open her mouth. Her eyes went wide. She started to pull back. He would not let her. Her hands came up and scratched at his face, and still he held her fast. The dagger fell forgotten from my grip.

"You vile devil!" I raged as I scrambled to pass through the hatch, only to double over with the effort, gasping from the pain I could no longer ignore. I groaned, as fresh warmth spread down my side in sharp contrast to the chill that crept across the rest of me. Gow's ball had more than found its mark.

Liam's eyes slid toward mine. The look in them stilled me. Without a word, they both ordered me to stay and begged me to trust. Though his mouth remained mated to our daughter's, his expression bore no sign of passion. It was madness, but I could not move, whether by compulsion, or the stupidity of love, I cannot say. I watched in horror as he blew a deep, sharp breath into her lungs. Only then did he release her head and move his away. Dreamlike, his hand reached up to his own face, caressing a trail through the blood marring his cheek. He looked at the crimson on his fingertips then turned a solemn gaze on his daughter.

"Trust me..." he murmured, the words holding the ghost of pleading. She just stared at him, her eyes wide. And after a moment, perhaps under the same spell as I, she nodded. He swiftly hugged her to him, brushed across her brow a more fatherly kiss, and slid her into the other selkie's arms.

Before my eyes, they disappeared below the water. They did not return. I shrieked and would have dove after but for Liam's arm locking fast about my waist. He had climbed from the hold swiftly, before I'd even realized. His grip tightened until agony drew a fog across my vision. I fought both it and him. He would not let me go any more than he had Katie.

Katie!

This...this is how love becomes hate.

"What? What?!" I snarled. "Was she too human for you?"

I twisted in his arms despite my growing pain and raked him as my daughter had. I bucked and thrashed and pummeled him as best I could, each effort weaker than the last. He simply took it, unmoving, anguish flooding his eyes.

Even fury could not sustain me long. Energy bled out of me. I went limp in his grasp and leaned as far out from him as I was able. I barely noticed that the storm still raged about us. It could not compare to the one within my heart.

My daughter. My daughter…gone by her own father's doing. A weak keening broke free from my throat.

Liam's grip shifted until he cradled me in a mockery of our loving days. I held myself stiff but did not fight. Heedless of the danger of our situation, he lowered us to the deck and sat with me nestled in his lap. His hands traced a slow path along the length of me, as if he sought to relearn familiar ground. It seduced me to a calm quite at odds with our surroundings. It lulled me into a twilight place where there was no storm or death or doubt. With each breath, my personal twilight crept deeper into night.

His hand stilled along my side. His head came up and his eyes looked hard into mine. Swiftly, he caught up the blade I had dropped to the deck. Carefully, he slit the whore's dress down the entire length and pushed it from my shoulders until it slid off my arms to the timbers. *Good riddin's*, I thought muzzily, glad to be freed from the hateful thing. No matter that I had nothing to replace it with. No matter.

"'Od's Blood!" Liam cursed and it sounded as if the words were uttered far away and softly. He clutched me even closer and all I felt was a twinge. He muttered more but the words were lost to me in the gloaming. Again he caressed me, leaving a trail of warmth from one end to the other.

I almost felt loved once more as he sang a softer, kinder selkie song into my ear. Not one of power and summoning, but one of comfort and entreaty. I took a step out of the darkness, struggled to conceive the anxiety in his words. I whimpered and my eyes drifted closed. With one hand, he pulled his sealskin toward us.

He stopped his singing and I felt his fingers upon my chin, gently bearing up. I kept my eyes closed, comfortable in my illusion, wanting just a moment longer of feeling cherished. I did not want to see what he did or did not think of me, even more human than the daughter he betrayed.

"Look at me, my love." His tone was as pleading as his gaze had been. I could not hold on to why I should loath him. I wanted to see his bonny face once more. It was an effort, but I opened my eyes to find him peering intently at me. Worry etched his brow and wore grooves along his sinful mouth. I was puzzled by what I saw in his gaze. Dared not even try to give it name, but damn my soul if my heart did not bound with love for him still.

"Trust me," he said earnestly. My outrage tried to rise up with the memories as he mirrored the words he'd said to my daughter. My love ignored it. In a daze, I nodded and watched as his hand pulled away. I gasped. Blood painted his hand red, though I could see no sign of injury upon him beyond slight scrapes. He reached up and again smeared the fresh blood beading his marred cheek, mingling it with what already coated his hand. This time he brought the fingers to my closed lips. My eyes widened and I shook my head.

"You must trust me! We have no time to waste!"

Whether that were true or not, the desperation woven through his words swayed me. My lips trembled as I parted them. His fingers slid inside and brushed my tongue with his lifeblood. I swallowed reflexively. Liam smiled and withdrew his fingers, only to replace them with his lips. My entire body quivered as he breathed into me as he had Katie.

With his mouth still locked over mine, he reached over and hurriedly drew the sealskin around my bare shoulders, then shifted me to cloak my naked legs as well. Confused, I crushed the thick, rich fur between my fingers. Such power he gave into my hands. Eyes solemn, he nodded, as if I had spoken the realization aloud. He then drew a final fold up over my head, leaving only my face bare.

I heard him whisper into my thoughts, *Blood of my blood, breath of my breath, flesh of my flesh. Be reborn.*

I gasped and twitched and reluctantly reconnected with my sense of self. Leaving the twilight completely, I conceived at once the aches running the length of my body, moaned at the burning fire consuming my side. Just a shade short of overwhelmed, my head lolled back and I turned frightened eyes upon my love. I had no strength to voice the questions that came to mind.

This time the world disappeared in a golden haze and an electric tingle swept over my body, like a promise of lightning in the air. In its wake, the pain was chased away.

Consciousness followed.

I woke to the sound of seals singing in triumph and joy. I woke to a small, furred body curled beside mine. I woke to the absence of pain. I woke to my own fur rippling as I basked in the warmth of a sun-baked rock. I woke to a dream: Liam's body nestled at my back, his flippers lazily caressing my side.

Seven years, my love, seven years I was bound by the curse of my kind to stay away, though I willed it not, Liam murmured sleepily into my thoughts. *But seven years have ended and nothing, not life nor death nor the devil Gow will keep me from your side e'er again.* Liam wrapped himself close about me as if he would be one with me forever.

Seven tears slid down to slick my fur and an unfamiliar bark escaped my throat, fill with both new joy and the remnants of old sorrow.

The cub beside me stirred, arched its head back in the graceful, impossible way of seals, and peered into my face with the eyes of my daughter.

My voice joined the selkie chorus.

By Silent Spell Caught

A Tale of the Last Celdraig

THE LAST OF THE DRAGONS CLIMBED THROUGH THE MISTS OF memory toward wakefulness.

She was Camirel, daughter of the Celdraig…daughter of the Last Mother. Transformed in the belly of the earth, she was no longer Man alone, but Dragon also. That sounded grand, but at the moment she lay naked, spent, and from the feel of it, possibly injured. It took an effort to focus her thoughts, to separate night-mare from dream from memory. Sleep had taken her — exhaustion really — but now instinct demanded she wake.

The spell that veiled her must have faded.

Camirel felt exposed. She worried about herself, but even more about the pouch secured about her waist, its contents more precious than her virtue. Though she had barely enough energy built back up to clothe herself with a thought, she made the effort anyway. Her temples pounded as she bent her will on donning

the simple cotton robe she usually called forth by magic when transitioning from dragon to human form. And none too soon....

As the soft, warm folds wrapped around her chilled flesh, hiding her body and the pouch from view, someone entered the cabin.

Unable to move, Cami listened to the heavy thud of footsteps crossing the floor. Wisps of memory became a bit more clear, borne upon the briny air, jostled by the shifting of the deck beneath her. She was aboard the *Devil's Get*. Its captain, the pirate Tulo, had something that didn't belong to him. She'd come to take it back. At the moment, she couldn't say if she'd succeeded. Or who approached her now. She tried to ready a defense only to awaken a piercing pain in the space behind her eyes. She lay there, praying to remain unnoticed, for she had no hope of protecting herself.

She prayed in vain.

Whoever it was stopped beside her; someone large and singularly disinclined to go away. A hard toe prodded her roughly until Cami slowly opened her eyes and let her head roll back. She could do nothing more. Not even groan with the effort. She lay there drained and battered, her shoulder throbbing.

In the moment it took to open her eyes, she assessed her surroundings. She lay in darkness barely lightened by the twilight that slipped past the broken windows of the captain's cabin. The sounds of the sea came to her ears: waves lapping against the outer hull, the splash of something breaking the skin of the water, airborne nocterns taunting the vessel, which now that she was conscious Camirel noted dipped and bobbed more than a ship at dock ought. The damaged window brought with it another memory: the captain falling dead at the hand of Camirel's nemesis, Malizia, just before the water witch escaped, breaking out through the glass. Even now the stench of Captain Tulo's voided body grew ripe.

Then the memory deepened...Malizia had slaughtered *all* of the crew.

Yet standing above Camirel was a deepening of the darkness, outlined in a half-familiar form. Before she could clear the fog from her thoughts, the shadow stooped and something more chilling than the metal it was made of clicked around her neck. Feebly, her hands rose to touch it and discovered a collar with no seam or hinge, sealed about her throat with pure magic.

The sickly pale glow of that connecting spell illuminated her captor, revealing a smooth, bald head marred on the right side by a three-inch gap to bare skull and a face mostly masked in dried blood. The man's nose was misshapen and his lower lip split near diagonal: Cragg, former first mate to the sack of meat poisoning the air…the only other who knew the secret of the runestones. He had aided Tulo in using them to steal spells from unwitting runecasters. But the stones were more than uncut gems; they were the cache Camirel had come to snatch away, safe now in the pouch she wore beneath her robe. They were not gems at all, but dragon young. Emberlings. She had vowed to see every one of them returned to their earthfire nests. Here stood a man with a vested interest in stopping her. Silently, she stared up at him, trying to read his expression, but the light from the spell rapidly faded leaving Camirel with no clue of his temper.

Until he spoke.

"Don't bother wishin' for death, *witch*. I don't have a bit of mercy in me." He swiftly stood. Then the heel of his booted foot came down upon her left forearm. The thud ended in a sharp crack.

Camirel discovered she could not voice a scream. She could not make any sound. She curled around her injured arm, taut with new-minted agony, pulse beating frantically a scale's thickness away from the edge of the razor-sharp control collar. That collar was kept from parting her skin only by a rune easily spoken away by her captor at any time, should it catch his whim. Morrow's corpse had worn such a collar…sunk deep into the flesh of his neck by the time she made his spirit's acquaintance.

Morrow! More mist lifted from Camirel's brain. Morrow…the unhoused soul of Captain Tulo's last — and final — victim. Cami had come to count him a friend. She longed to reach down to see if she still retained the emberling he was bound to, among those she had come to steal way, but she dared not beneath Cragg's harsh gaze.

"You'll not catch me again with your 'casting," the surviving pirate muttered as he moved toward the captain's remains. With little care and no ceremony, the pirate stripped the corpse of all valuables, and then dumped the body overboard through the broken window. He then left the cabin with his loot, not bothering to close the door. Cami soon heard the distant splash of Malizia's other victims being consigned to the sea.

Cami stared at the wreckage of the window and then toward the unbarred door.

Clearly, Cragg saw her as no physical threat even as he assumed silencing her would hobble her magic.

He was wrong. She was no weak-powered runecaster, needing to speak or write her runes. Even with her personal energy nigh spent, magic for her was but a thought and the tapping of a ready power source.

Despite her weariness, despite her pain, she reached out her senses and drew upon the earthfire, called it to her, and ordered her thoughts. The earthfire answered, but did not come, *could* not come to her summons. In that moment, Cami sensed the depth of her ill-fated luck: they were no longer secure at dock, but afloat at sea, surrounded by water, the antithesis of her fire. Anywhere but on open water she could call on the mage energy generated by all life. Here she was too far from the earth and the fire at its core. Here, without personal energy to draw on, she was crippled, like any other mortal. If she were in dragon form it would not matter how much water surrounded her.

Of course, if she were in dragon form, she wouldn't have been captured.

Her head fell back in a silent wail, the last of her energy spent.

M'lady…Camirel…by the First Mother, girl, speak to me!

The voice whispering direct into her mind held a desperate edge. She was tempted not to answer, to retreat back into oblivion. But compassion and duty united to prevent her from such a selfish act. She half opened her eyes and looked about her. It was still night and darkness filled the room, but for a few patches of moonlight.

Camirel… the voice repeated.

As Cami came more awake her annoyance gave way to deep-seated relief. The voice belonged to Morrow, and through the touch of his thoughts she sensed that he and the emberlings were safe in the pouch she wore beneath her robe. Their fate weighed upon her.

She did not move. She could not speak. But there was no such governor on her thoughts.

What know you, my friend?

Morrow's relief was palpable. *Once they saw what was done, and how, the constables fled the ship and cut it loose,* he told her. *Apparently trusting the tide to take care of the matter, rather than risk getting tangled with what wrought such slaughter. They knew nothing of yourself or Malizia. They certainly knew nothing of the runestones, or they would not have acted with such haste. None came aboard any further than the main deck before debarking with all swiftness.*

Interesting, and something she had not considered when she'd planned to wait out the authorities. *What of the pirates?*

They are dead, but for Cragg. Though why he isn't, is a wonder.

Camirel agreed. She had gotten a good look at that gash up close. If he didn't attend to Malizia's handiwork, neglect would not be long in finishing the deed.

Cami wondered what Cragg intended. Other than the collar, he had not bound her, nor had he stripped her of her belongings. Her clothes remained in place and the pouch of emberlings still safe beneath them. Of course, it would take a mage stronger than she to even sense the pouch and its contents were there, let along separate the two. Not many could claim such power.

That woke in her a chilling thought: *He thinks it was me. He thinks I was the witch that maimed him and slaughtered the captain and crew.*

Oh, Great Mother! Alarm welled up and Cami was frantic for a way free of her predicament. Her breath raced and her throat locked tight as every muscle tensed. There was no telling what vengeance the sailor planned or when he would strike. She'd already had a taste of his cruelty. She forced the panic down, walled it off in a back portion of her brain and refused it any attention. It would not serve her now. She needed to rebuild her resources and figure out a plan. But first she must get herself together.

What is wrong? Morrow asked.

My arm, she murmured back. *I must tend to it or we have no hope of getting free.*

She sensed uneasiness in Morrow's thoughts. Some hesitation. But when he did not speak again, she discounted it and went about the goal she'd set for herself.

Moving with a care for her broken arm, Camirel sat up and scanned the cabin, looking for something to bind up her injury. Nothing lay nearby and none of the captain's effects visible in the moonlight were even remotely suited. Cursing the need, she drew herself to her feet, her good arm gripping one of the cabin's bracings. Iced drops of sweat beaded her brow by the time she was upright and her teeth gritted against the pain. The collar alone kept her from the humiliation of whimpering. As much as she was able, she followed the wall, carefully skirting the bed and the heavy cedar chest bolted to the deck beside it. Her good arm steadied her as she made her way around the room, searching until she came back to the point where she'd started with nothing to show for the effort but a bit of fruit, some travel bread of higher quality than hard tack, and the dregs of a bottle of wine. She set all that aside for later. For now, her stomach roiled with each step; between the pain of her arm and the lingering stench it was a wonder she had not already heaved. Likely she would have, if not for the fresh air coming in off the open sea.

The thought brought her head rearing up, her eyes locked upon the broken window with its long, straight lengths of pane no longer needed for their given task. If her startled laugh had had voice there would have been a touch of the hysterical about it. Camirel abandoned the wall and made straight for the window, only to stumble as the ship lurched over a swell. She came down on her bad arm, bone grated against bone. The loose splinters and jagged ends cut into her flesh until she feared they would break through the skin. The roiling in her gut immediately turned to retching, though precious little came up. For a time, she blacked out. Resurfacing through a cascade of pain, unsure of how long she'd been unconscious, she found herself in a puddle of sick that was little more than bile, the pain flashing colored jags across her vision.

Ah! she cried out in the silence of her thoughts as tears streamed down her cheeks. Her features contorted with the agony.

Camirel! Morrow answered her cry, his tone a mix of concern and frustration.

Give me a minute. Even her mental voice sounded gritted, faint.

No, Camirel, he insisted. *Listen to me. The stones…* and here the hesitation crept back in, *…the ruby-colored runesto…emberlings, they are marked with a spell for healing.*

For a moment she knew pure hope despite the dire situation. And yet, Morrow had hesitated. She had to wonder why.

Morrow…what happens to the stones once the magic has been spent?

Silence.

Morrow? Pain made her tone harsh.

I don't know…until you told me they were emberlings, it didn't matter. I didn't even know what they really were. She could not dispute that. No one beside herself knew that runestones were actually dragon young torn from the earth before their time. Their magical nature was what made it possible for Tulo to capture spells upon them.

Every curse she'd ever heard streamed through Camirel's mind. Injured, she stood little chance of getting *any* of the emberlings to safety, but she was sworn to care for and protect them all. In her battle with Malizia, one of the emberlings had been destroyed. Cami still felt the cry of that lost soul. Dare she risk that using the imprinted rune would do harm to the one it was bound to? Dare she not? Was she to lose them all, or perhaps just one? The pain grew unbearable; the uncertainty even worse.

What... she had to force the thought. *What is the trigger?*

He gave her the word.

It sat heavy in her mind. Morrow did not push her as she huddled in a pool of moonlight halfway to the window, considering the unsavory option he'd offered. As she pondered, the square of moonlight traveled across the floor, leaving her again in darkness. The sounds of bodies being fed to the sea had long faded and the smells of sick were lessened, if not gone, thanks to the breeze. And still, though hours passed, Cami made no move to use the trigger word or even bind her arm by more mundane means. She could sense Morrow patiently waiting. In a way she wished he'd push her, that she would not feel the blame so heavily should her fears be proved out. But no...it would not matter. The responsibility and any corresponding guilt were and always would be her own.

Camirel thought the trigger word.

One minute, then two passed and she wondered had she gotten something wrong. Hard to imagine, mind to mind, but she was pain-dazed and exhausted. She considered 'uttering' it again, only her arm began to tingle and then all she could think to do was scream until her mind rang with a silent cry as unseen forces pulled muscle and bone taut and straight, and the fire of the 'casting fused the very cells back into place. Cold ache was replaced by the lingering heat of that momentary burn. Camirel's knuckles popped when her hand involuntarily flexed with the healing. Even the last vestiges of pain in her shoulder were no more.

Bind it.

Cami jerked at the unexpected order, making no move to obey.

Bind it, now! Morrow snapped at her again. *Or do you wish Cragg to know you have the means to work magic?*

First Mother help her if the pirate learned that! What a price he could command for a controlled runecaster!

She nodded sharply in agreement. Moving with much surer steps toward the casement, Camirel noted that the collar began to vibrate uncomfortably the closer she approached the opening. She growled soundlessly and her stomach clenched as she realized what that meant for her, and why she'd not been secured. Stopping two feet from theoretical freedom, she stretched out her arms and broke off two lengths of damaged pane roughly equal to her forearm. As she did so, her mouth opened wide and her breath seized in her chest as she felt the sting of several layers of skin about her neck parting beneath the collar's edge. Hastily she jerked herself back and thought all manner of dire thoughts at the one responsible. She grimaced and reflected, *It's important to know one's boundaries.*

Morrow's response was a rude sound deep in her mind. Cami almost laughed.

By touch and faint moonlight, she carefully examined her prize, working away a splinter or two before deeming the wood serviceable for her needs. Setting them down she then turned her attention toward the bindings she would need. Her gaze lingered on the captain's bed. Tulo struck her as the type that had commanded creature comforts. She was not wrong in this. Tugging the heavy down covering from the bed to the floor, with satisfaction she considered the costly silk sheets beneath. Cragg could get a nice bit of gold for them, if he weren't inclined to enjoy them himself….

With no small amount of glee, she squandered a bit of regained energy to briefly transform her fingers to dragon talons, the better to shred the sheets, not caring if the sound of tearing cloth traveled. Now for the binding…. It was awkward, but she managed to sandwich her arm between the splints and wrap it tight with strips of silk until no flesh showed, employing her right hand, teeth, and both knees to get the deed accomplished. With a final strip of silk, she made a sling to support her arm, a reminder really, that it was not to be used. As for pain; there was no need to feign discomfort once she was done. Healed her arm might be, but not without lingering effect.

With that thought came a reminder of what she had risked.

Taking a deep breath, she turned her senses to the pouch of emberlings, tried to feel if the life had gone out of any one of them. But it was as if her mage senses were encased in cloudy ice. Or perhaps it was that she could not tell with the emberlings jumbled together so closely; if so, she did not dare to draw them out to inspect them one by one. No telling when the pirate would return.

Can you sense him, Morrow?

The spirit grew a little distant as he focused elsewhere, searching for Cragg. *Enough to tell he's below, but not what he's doing.*

Weary and aching and no small amount heartsick, Cami turned and considered the door. There was a runelock on it. When she'd first entered the chamber (what seemed another lifetime ago), she'd had to shield herself and wait for Tulo to show so she could follow him past the safeguard. She had had no choice, not knowing the trigger word. She rued the fact that she herself had prevented the door from closing then, thinking she might need a quick escape. If she had let it close behind her, she might have saved herself a broken arm.

Then again…maybe not.

Does Cragg know the trigger for the runelock?

Tulo didn't trust anyone and he didn't share power, Morrow answered. *Safe to say, I think, that the answer is no.*

Dare she trust Morrow was right? Truth was it didn't matter. Cami was so spent she trembled all over and her eyes now showed her the world in only black and white and shades of grey. Again bracing herself against the wall, she made her way to the door and closed it firmly, but softly. Her heart did not slow its pace until her mage senses confirmed the rune engaged. Once it did, she nearly slumped to the ground as the tension went out of her; only by sheer will did she manage to keep her feet. At the least she would have warning should Cragg return for her while she slept. That would have to be enough for now.

You must eat, Morrow said, jarring her from the haze she'd settled into.

I don't think I can, she answered. *I'm too tired.*

Sleep alone will not restore you, m'lady.

Camirel, she reminded him, as if his use of her name now that she'd granted it was more vital to her than food.

He growled and she could feel the weight of his regard, no matter he had no physical form. She sighed, or thought to anyway, and knew that he was right. Standing propped against the wall, she ate a quarter portion of what she had found earlier and limited herself to two swigs of the harsh wine. The rest she tucked inside the chest for later.

With her last moments of consciousness, she tugged the bedcovering from where she'd dropped it earlier and made a nest for herself between the cedar chest and the wall. She fell asleep practically before she crawled inside.

Her sleep was disturbed by the sound of chopping.

Thunk. Crack! Thunk. Crack! echoed in her dreams as the ax head entered and was torn from solid wood.

Camirel huddled deep beneath the down and tried to ignore the noise, annoyed that one of the Brothers would do the chore at such an impolite hour. True, the Order that had taken her in and offered her sanctuary at Mabet after her parents' death was an industrious one, but they were generally more considerate of those not required to rise so early. She shifted and tried to draw the blankets closer against the chill when an aching twinge in her arm served the last clue to her memory. *Thunk! Crack!* The cabin door split with the sound of finality, just as Cami shook off sleep. She stared defiantly at the pirate as the splintered remnants fell away.

So much for the runelock….

Cragg stalked through the wreckage to stand over her, ax still half hefted in his right hand. At some time in the night he'd stitched closed his wounds with thick, raw silk thread. Except for the bruising, his face was stark white in comparison. His eyes blazed. Something about the intent look he gave her made her uneasy. "Move, *witch*," he snapped at her. "Before we lose the tide." She wanted to snap back. Just as well she couldn't as the impulse was hardly wise. As she scrambled to her feet, he grabbed her unbound arm the moment she came within reach and propelled her toward the door, following fast on her heels.

The morning light near blinded her as she stumbled out on to the deck. The air was chilled and the waves choppy, making it hard for her to find her legs so shortly drawn from sleep. She stopped, blinking and swaying as she looked around her, only to be pushed toward where the longboat waited to be lowered. Cragg had already loaded the craft with a number of casks and sacks, the contents of which she couldn't identify, but on the deck of the ship waited a more substantial pile of sturdy, well-sealed containers, all lashed together with thick, stout rope, and anchored to a buoy.

Morrow, what's going on? she asked the spirit, who'd spent more time aboard a pirate ship than she.

That's his lagan, he answered. *Loot he wants to salvage but can't take with him. He's going to sink it with the ship and that buoy will help him find the stuff when he comes back for it.*

Now that Morrow mentioned it, she could smell guncotton on the air. She looked over her shoulder at the ship and nearly jumped back. Cragg stood practically on top of her, a burning brand in his hand and a sack strapped across his back. "Get in the longboat," he ordered.

It wasn't like she could argue, but she also wasn't above a bit of revenge. Gathering the tiniest bit of her restored mage energy she thought a rune of unbinding, ensuring the buoy no longer tethered the treasure.

"Ah! I thought so!" The grin on Cragg's face struck Camirel like a cannon round passing through her gut. "You aren't the only one what has the Sense, witch. Who is it you figure made that little trinket you're wearin'? Certainly wasn't that ass, Tulo, or his slave 'casters." His gaze took on a leer. "I felt whatever you wrought in the night. More fool you, not usin' it to try and get free. Now I know enough to keep you in my sight, at least for the short while it matters. Try one thing false and you can consider the trigger spoken. I value my skin more than any profit you may bring." He paused then and looked her up and down in frank assessment. "I thank you in particular, though…you just trebled the price I'll settle on you and those stones you think you're hidin' once we hit shore."

Unable to yell or curse or scream at him to her satisfaction, Camirel spat upon him, her face surely twisted with the rage and desperation she felt inside. Cragg only laughed and cuffed her hard until she stumbled against the bulwark, just catching herself before she tumbled over the rail. "Get in the boat!" he roared after her. With little choice otherwise, she scrambled to obey, pressing herself as far back as the goods would allow as she watched him climb aboard, tossing the brand to the far side of the ship as he left the deck. Camirel barely had time to wrap herself around the lashings holding the cargo in place when she noticed Cragg draw a machete from the bilge of the boat and with a quick slash, severed the winch line holding the longboat aloft.

It hurt screaming with no sound. It was as if her body strained all the harder to be heard and she paid the price for its failure. Cragg just laughed all the way.

As the longboat splashed down into the sea, taking on a good bit of water in the process, he tossed her a bilge bucket.

"You might as well do away with those bandages and get to work. By the way you're wrapped around that rope, it's fair clear now what you spent yourself on in the night."

Camirel had never used her magic to do harm. The very thought was anathema to her, as it would have been to all Celdraig. Just as well. Her expression must have given her away as she remotely considered doing so now.

"Shall I say it?" Cragg murmured, leaning close, his thick, callused finger running just below the collar ringing her neck. Her scored skin stung at his touch. "One word and I'll finish what you've just barely started here." His finger came away with dried flecks of her blood speckling the tip. Cami schooled her expression to remain neutral and slowly shook her head.

"Start bailing, then," Cragg said. "I don't fancy soaking my feet all the way to landfall."

Presuming her complete compliance with his order, Cragg applied himself to the oars with haste, long, deep pulls sending them flying across the mostly calm water as fast as his well-muscled arms could manage. They were barely far enough away when the ship blew. Concussion waves swamped the longboat, sinking their draft a little deeper.

At a hard glance from her captor Cami bent more energetically to her task.

With care, but less than half a thought on the process, she dumped each bucket over the edge. With the rest she barraged Morrow with questions. *Did you know this? Did you know the man was a 'caster?*

Morrow's mental tone sounded both rueful and wry. *When I was graced with my collar they'd knocked me cold first with the runestone from Tulo's dagger. There were no others come after me until yourself.*

The spirit fell silent and Camirel was distracted by her own thoughts.

The dagger…she'd forgotten the dagger! Set into the pommel was one of her emberlings. Cragg had pocketed it with the rest of Tulo's belongings before he'd tossed the body to the sea. She had to get it if she could.

She took a quick moment to assess the water level in the bottom of the boat. Without a thimble she wasn't likely to bail out much more, the level being below the rim of her current bucket. She set it aside and scurried to the far side of the boat, propping herself against the cargo and looking out at the churning sea.

Tension knotted her gut at what she saw. The waves caused by the sinking ship should have exhausted by now. With no obvious weather darkening the sky, the choppy look of the wake unnerved her. In the distance, she thought she caught the occasional wisp of vapor rising from the water…. Such spoke of power beneath the waves. But what the source? Dare she hope…? There were places where the ocean floor rose to meet the waves, rather than the other way around. If they passed above one of those fault-lines, and the underwater volcanoes such generally caused, she would have a chance at tapping into the earthfire.

Reeling out a bit of personal energy, Cami probed beneath the water, only to find herself frustrated. She could not tell. It was like her senses were hobbled.

The rogue never gave me reason, that I can recall, to believe he was a runecaster, Morrow finally spoke again, his tone reflective. *I have delved as deep as I am able into memory and there is none that I can hold up to say 'I should have known.'*

The sudden resumption of the previous conversation startled Camirel from her efforts. It took her a moment to focus on what he said.

Of course, the collar dampens the mage sense, which you may have noticed, and I was never much around him when I wasn't working runes myself. But I think it is telling that Cragg was the only one of the crew who knew the secret of the runestones and was involved in their creation.

Another silent sigh rose from Cami. *Can you tell me anything about the collar?*

Not much. I was not strong enough to fight it, or even test it. Mine allowed me speech and movement, only holding over me the dire threat that came with disobedience. I did not have the boundaries set upon me that you do. But perhaps that is because the villains had time to prepare for my ambush, but not for yours? Thus he had to bind you in more ways to make up for other weakness in the runes?

Her teeth clenched behind her smooth expression. This was all supposition. She needed to know more.

What if you look closer at this one? Perhaps you can tell what I cannot.

She felt a gentle probing from Morrow.

It does feel different, but I cannot say how as I did not know the composition of my own.

Her frustration ran deep and it was her turn to fall silent. It wasn't Morrow's fault, but that scarcely mattered given her current mood. She had not taken up her charge from the Last Mother to so utterly fail. With less than a handful of emberlings interred there was not even the hope her efforts might be enough were she to fall now to this foe.

Morrow, she said, after long moments of thought. *Do you know what it is made of?*

Again the probing.

Steel, he finally answered. *Nothing more than steel. I can see the runes upon it as I never could with mortal eyes and they do nothing more than hold the edge from your skin or, be the trigger word spoken or set boundaries breached, draw the elements of the metal closer to one another, sinking the blade into your flesh.*

Pleasant thought, that. Camirel figured she could have done without confirmation of those particulars, no matter that she'd already known.

Morrow went on, *A separate rune keeps you silent, most likely because he knew nothing of your skill. There is another to keep you from sketching runes, but as you don't need to, it has not hindered you.*

She barely 'heard' him, her mind locked on the matter of the steel. Only…it did her no good *now*, but what if she had a chance to transform? Common steel, even magicked, was no proof against dragon scales, not with earthfire strengthening them beyond the hardness of diamonds. Runespelled or not, the steel would shatter the moment she drew the 'fire and took on the form.

Again, it did her no good now…

…but let her be right about the approaching source of earthfire, and Cragg would soon piss himself in the face of the Dragon in her.

She let the prospect smolder as she watched the surface of the sea for more signs of sub-aquatic venting. There was a feel to the air that gave her hope, a subtle vibration against her skin that had nothing to do with fear or runes or rage.

Finally, she spied that for which she searched: a massive plume of steam rising from the surface of the water, as like the wisps she noted earlier as a whale was to a new-spawned fish. She lurched to her feet and turned toward the glorious earthfire rising from below.

Behind her she heard Cragg curse as she off-balanced the boat. She sensed him falter and jerk, but did not let her attention waver from her goal. Camirel locked her eyes on the vapors. Ahead lurked an underwater volcano; the purest source of earthfire to be had upon the sea. A few more strokes, just a few more, and she would be near enough to draw upon its energy.

As they drifted closer Cami began to gather the trailing wisps to her.

"What the hell are you doing?" She felt Cragg finally lunge for her.

Camirel grimaced, unable to retort. With her left hand, she gripped the rope binding the cargo to steady herself against the lurching of the boat; with the other, she yanked one of her splints out of its binding, leaving splinters of wood in her flesh, but gaining what she could in the way of a projectile. Closing her eyes, she resumed drawing the earthfire from the superheated, ambient air. It wasn't quite enough to change, but it was more than sufficient to send the hardened wood spearing toward the pirate. As a weapon, it had no hope of even scratching Cragg's skin, but as a distraction…just enough! He batted the projectile away. The motion unbalanced him a vital moment as he regained his center.

And then…they were there.

Though he no longer stroked the oars, their momentum brought the longboat over the slope of the volcano's cone. Camirel's back arched and she gasped without sound as 'fire suddenly flooded the empty spaces within her that had been aching for its burn. She barely heard Cragg's startled cry as the power filled her up to the limit of her human form, and then she drew more.

Her skin throbbed and her head thrashed. For a moment, the sensations overwhelmed her, like sleep-numbed limbs that pulsed with the return of blood flow, only hotter. Somewhere distant in her thoughts Morrow whispered, talked her down, reminded her of her goal, her purpose beyond that glorious moment of restoration. He warned her as Cragg uttered the rune holding the collar from her flesh. A growl rumbled from her throat, deepening in pitch as it went on. Newly grounded and steeped in power, Camirel guided it with her mind, thought 'Dragon' and put on that skin, that shape. As always, her clothing disappeared and the pouch holding the emberlings sank magically beneath her dragon hide, protected and secure. The tightening steel, however, shattered against her scales as she rose on the surging plume of ash and gas brought to the surface by her draw upon the volcano's power.

Freed, she bellowed her challenge to the world.

She barely heard the frightened cry rise from the longboat below.

Camirel spread the dual sets of sail-like wings that had replaced her human arms and bugled a triumphant call no spell could silence. The frilled vanes that graced her elegant head fanned about her and she briefly hovered there in full glory, tail thrashing and underbelly reflecting the blues and greens of the sea. Arching her now-sinuous neck, she gazed at the man crouching in her shadow.

Pivoting with ease on a wingtip, she swooped down and grasped Cragg carefully in her claws, bearing him up until he trailed beneath her. She then arrowed toward an island she'd sighted in the distance; an island seemingly untouched by humankind, but surely capable of sustaining one lone man.

She was not unmoved by his frantic thrashing. A glance down revealed his attempts to sketch runes upon the wind, only she flew too swiftly for him to complete them, leaving a trail of disjointed magic in her wake. She took some satisfaction in absorbing the lingering energy, which Cragg surely sensed, given his bellowed rage.

"Don't bother wishing for death, *sir…*" she said, human words coming without difficulty from her dragon's muzzle. "I am sure you will suffer much more having to live with my mercy." And with those words, she dropped him none too gently upon the hot sands of the deserted beach.

Are you sure it is wise to leave him breathing? Morrow cautioned.

Camirel sighed, and then snarled in frustration. *No, not at all. However, I am not such as he; I have no choice. But first, I claim what is mine.*

She reached out with razor talons and tore open the sack secured across the pirate's back. Out tumbled valuables looted from the ship, Tulo's belongings among them. With a triumphant roar, Camirel snatched up the sheathed dagger bearing the emberling pommel and soared away across the sky, heading for the volcano, whose maw led straight to the belly of the First Mother.

And the last of dragonkind returned her hard-won emberlings to their nests. All but the one to which Morrow was bound.

Danielle Ackley-McPhail

Award-winning author and editor Danielle Ackley-McPhail has worked both sides of the publishing industry for longer than she cares to admit. In 2014 she joined forces with husband Mike McPhail and friend Greg Schauer to form her own publishing house, eSpec Books (www.especbooks.com).

Her published works include six novels, *Yesterday's Dreams*, *Tomorrow's Memories*, *Today's Promise*, *The Halfling's Court*, *The Redcaps' Queen*, and *Baba Ali and the Clockwork Djinn*, written with Day Al-Mohamed. She is also the author of the solo collections *A Legacy of Stars*, *Consigned to the Sea*, *Flash in the Can*, and *Transcendence*, the non-fiction writers' guide, *The Literary Handyman,* and is the senior editor of the *Bad-Ass Faeries* anthology series, *Gaslight & Grimm*, *Dragon's Lure*, and *In an Iron Cage*. Her short stories are included in numerous other anthologies and collections.

She is a member of Broad Universe, a writer's organization focusing on promoting the works of women authors in the speculative genres.

In addition to her literary acclaim, she crafts and sells original costume horns under the moniker The Hornie Lady, at literary conventions, on commission, and wholesale.

Danielle lives in New Jersey with husband and fellow writer, Mike McPhail and three extremely spoiled cats. She can be found on Facebook (Danielle Ackley-McPhail) and Twitter (DMcPhail, BadAssFaeries, eSpecBooks, and TheHornieLady).
To learn more about her work, visit www.sidhenadaire.com and www.especbooks.com.

Also Featured

Val Griswold-Ford is the author of the Dark Horseman novels *Not Your Father's Horseman*, *Dark Moon Seasons* and *Last Rites*, all from Dragon Moon Press. She is also the co-editor of *The Complete Guide to Writing Fantasy: the Opus Magnus* (with Tee Morris) and *The Complete Guide to Writing Fantasy: The Author's Grimoire* (with Lai Zhao), also from Dragon Moon Press, and has self-published the short e-novella *Snow* and, most recently, the short story *Convoy*. She has published several short stories in various anthologies online and in print, and is owned by three cats. She and her husband live in New Hampshire with said cats. You can find her at www.vg-ford.com or on Twitter as @vg_ford.

Brenda Cooper writes science fiction and fantasy novels and short stories. Her most recent novel is *The Diamond Deep*, which came out in October of 2013 from Pyr. It's book two of a two-book series that started with *The Creative Fire*. She has seven novels out numerous short stories. Brenda is also a technology professional and a futurist, and publishes non-fiction on the environment and the future.

See her website at www.brenda-cooper.com.

Brenda lives in the Pacific Northwest in a household with three people, three dogs, more than three computers, and only one TV in it.

D. B. Jackson is the award-winning author of fifteen novels and the occasional short story. His most recent novels, *Thieftaker*

and *Thieves' Quarry*, written under the D.B. Jackson pen name (www.DBJackson-Author.com), are the first volumes of the *Thief-taker Chronicles*, a series set in pre-Revolutionary Boston that combines elements of urban fantasy, mystery, and historical fiction. The third volume, *A Plunder of Souls*, will be published in 2014.

Writing as David B. Coe (www.DavidBCoe.com) he has published the *LonTobyn Chronicle* trilogy, the *Winds of the Forelands* quintet and the *Blood of the Southlands* trilogy. He has also written the novelization of director Ridley Scott's movie, *Robin Hood*, starring Russell Crowe.

Misty Massey is the author of Mad Kestrel (Tor Books), a rollicking adventure of magic on the high seas which was nominated for the 2010 SCASL Book Award. Misty is one of the featured writers on Magical Words.net. Misty's short fiction has appeared in the Rum and Runestones, Dragon's Lure and The Big Bad II. When she's not writing, Misty lifts weights and studies Middle Eastern dance, performing in shows around the Carolinas.

Alma Alexander was born in a country which no longer exists on the maps, has lived and worked in seven countries on four continents (and in cyberspace!), has climbed mountains, dived in coral reefs, flown small planes, swum with dolphins, touched two-thousand-year-old tiles in a gate out of Babylon. She is a novelist, anthologist and short story writer who currently shares her life between the Pacific Northwest of the USA (where she lives with her husband and two cats) and the wonderful fantasy worlds of her own imagination. You can find out more about Alma on her websites (www.AlmaAlexander.org and www.AlmaAlexander.com).